Want to add some laughter, adventure, and spice to your life? Check out all three of Ann Charles' mystery series:

A DEADWOOD MYSTERY

Stop by for a visit to the Old West town of Deadwood, South Dakota—the Ann Charles version. This USA Today bestselling, multiple award-winning humorous mystery series is packed with quirky characters, nail-biting paranormal suspense, and spicy romance. Violet Parker will have to hang on tight and stick to her guns through the crazy adventures in store for her. Thank goodness she has a lot of gumption and help from her friends.

A DIG SITE MYSTERY

Welcome to the jungle—the steamy Maya jungle that is, filled with ancient ruins and deadly secrets. Quint Parker, renowned photojournalist (and lousy amateur detective), is in for a whirlwind of adventure and suspense as he and archaeologist, Dr. Angélica García, get tangled up in mysteries from the past and present at exotic dig sites. Loaded with action and laughs, along with all sorts of steamy heat, these two will keep you sweating along with them as they do their best to make it out of the jungle alive in every book.

A JACKRABBIT JUNCTION MYSTERY

Down here at the Dancing Winnebagos RV Park in Jackrabbit Junction, Arizona, Claire Morgan and her rabble-rousing sisters are really good at getting into trouble—BIG trouble (the land your butt in jail kind of trouble). This rowdy, laugh-aloud mystery series is packed with action, suspense, adventure, and relationship snafus. Full of colorful characters and twisted up plots, the stories of the Morgan sisters will keep you wondering what kind of a screwball mess they are going to land in next.

For more information about Ann and her books, check out her website, as well as the reader reviews for her books on Amazon, Barnes & Noble, and Goodreads

Also by Ann Charles

Deadwood Mystery Series
Nearly Departed in Deadwood (Book 1)
Optical Delusions in Deadwood (Book 2)
Dead Case in Deadwood (Book 3)
Better Off Dead in Deadwood (Book 4)
An Ex to Grind in Deadwood (Book 5)
Meanwhile, Back in Deadwood (Book 6)
A Wild Fright in Deadwood (Book 7)

Short Stories from the Deadwood Mystery Series
Deadwood Shorts: Seeing Trouble
Deadwood Shorts: Boot Points
Deadwood Shorts: Cold Flame
Deadwood Shorts: Tequila & Time

Jackrabbit Junction Mystery Series
Dance of the Winnebagos (Book 1)
Jackrabbit Junction Jitters (Book 2)
The Great Jackalope Stampede (Book 3)
The Rowdy Coyote Rumble (Book 4)
The Wild Turkey Tango (Novella 4.5)

Goldwash Mystery Series (a future series)
The Old Man's Back in Town (Short Story)

Dig Site Mystery Series
Look What the Wind Blew In (Book 1)
Make No Bones About It (Book 2)

Coming Next from Ann Charles

Deadwood Mystery Series
Title TBA (Book 8)

Dear Reader,

One of the things I've wanted to do since I wrote *Nearly Departed in Deadwood,* the first book in my Deadwood Mystery Series, was to write several short stories that give the backstory of the characters and/or the setting. I chose not to include these bits of backstory in the actual novels because I didn't want to slow the pace. Also, due to the fact that we're always in Violet's head, some of the short stories I want to write and share would be difficult to play out on the pages of the novels.

This series of short ebooks will be released in between the regular length Deadwood novels and will offer what I hope to be fun insights to gobble up, kind of like those mini-sized candy bars and MoonPies. Rather than blather on about my random ideas, crazy antics, and diabolical plans, I present to you the first Deadwood Shorts ebook: *Seeing Trouble.*

Seeing Trouble offers answers to some of the questions I've received from fans about how Violet Parker ended up as a single mother of twins. It was originally titled *Dear Diary in Deadwood* and was part of a Valentine's Day anthology with several other authors' works. In addition to this short story, I've included the original character interview I did with Violet prior to writing the first book that introduced us to her wild world. I threw in a couple of Deadwood illustrations by C.S. Kunkle that were created for my original website. I have also included several images that show the progression of the cover design for *Nearly Departed in Deadwood,* from the first working cover I created after finishing the first draft, through several contenders drawn by C.S. Kunkle, to the final product that you see today. Finally, I added a short story called *Candy Lover* that I pulled from my story vault. It has nothing to do with Violet and Deadwood, but it's a story that I felt might put a smile on your face.

I hope you enjoy this first ebook in the Deadwood Shorts series.

As Old Man Harvey would say, "Don't squat with your spurs on."

Ann Charles

DEADWOOD

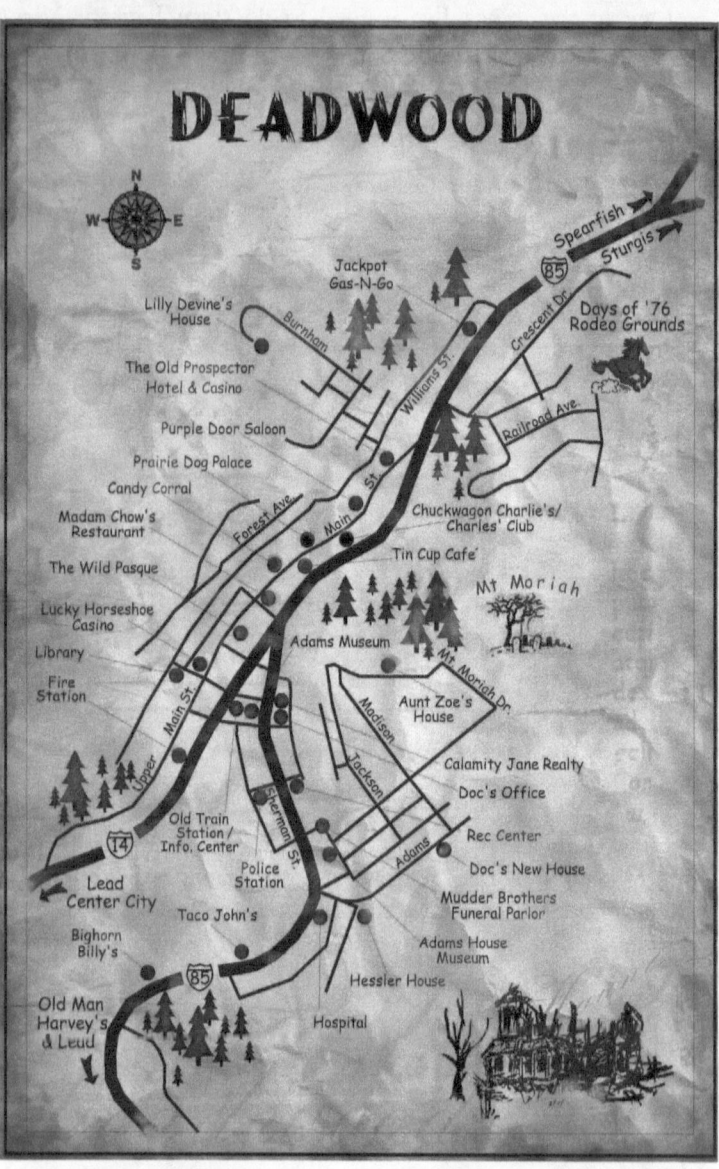

Lilly Devine's House

The Old Prospector Hotel & Casino

Purple Door Saloon

Prairie Dog Palace

Candy Corral

Madam Chow's Restaurant

The Wild Pasque

Lucky Horseshoe Casino

Library

Fire Station

Jackpot Gas-N-Go

Burnham

Williams St.

Main St.

Forest Ave.

Upper Main St.

Spearfish

Sturgis

Crescent Dr.

Railroad Ave.

Days of '76 Rodeo Grounds

Chuckwagon Charlie's/ Charlies' Club

Tin Cup Cafe'

Mt Moriah

Adams Museum

Mt. Moriah Dr.

Aunt Zoe's House

Madison

Jackson

Calamity Jane Realty

Doc's Office

Rec Center

Doc's New House

Mudder Brothers Funeral Parlor

Adams House Museum

Sherman St.

Adams

Old Train Station / Info. Center

Police Station

Lead Center City

Taco John's

Bighorn Billy's

Old Man Harvey's & Lead

Hessler House

Hospital

DEADWOOD
Shorts

Seeing Tr/Double

Ann Charles

Deadwood Shorts: Seeing Trouble

Cover Design by Sharon Benton, Q42 Designs
Cover Photo by Bob Wilson, Frogworks Photography
Illustrations by C.S. Kunkle

Special thanks to my beta readers extraordinaire. You all rock!

E-book ISBN-13: 978-1-940364-01-8
Print ISBN-:13: 978-1-940364-50-6

Seeing Trouble

Deadwood, South Dakota

H ey, Mom," said Addy, my nine-year-old daughter, as she burst through my bedroom doorway. "Elvis found this old book in the basement."

She held out a book I hadn't seen in over a decade—my old diary. The upper corner of the cover had been pecked, leaving it tattered.

Elvis was my daughter's pet chicken. Long story short, she planned to save the animal kingdom one pet at a time. Elvis was just another in Addy's long line of birds, mammals, rodents, fish, and amphibious creatures. I'd drawn a line at the garter snake. Indiana Jones wasn't the only one with a loathing for things that go slither in the night ... or day.

"It has a cool little lock on it. It must be a diary," Addy said, holding up a paperclip. "Can I try to pop it open?"

I inspected the lock for scratches, wondering if she already had and was just covering her ass by asking. "You know how diaries work, Addy. They are for the owners' eyes only."

"But we don't know whose diary this is. It could be the long-lost diary of Calamity Jane."

Being that we lived in Deadwood, which was famous for its history of gold rushes and gunfights, my daughter tended to think that anything older than she belonged to some famous historical figure. Take the old rusted spur her twin brother Layne, my very own wanna-be archaeologist, dug up in the yard last week. She was certain it had belonged to Wild Bill Hickok.

"We do know whose diary this is, Addy. It's mine."

"Are you sure? It looks really old."

Shut it, child. "Isn't it time for you to take Elvis for a walk?"

"What did you write about in it?" she asked, ignoring my attempt at distraction.

Your father. "Just some thoughts on life and growing up."

"You should let me read it. I might learn something of value."

It was ironic how whenever she wanted to get her way, she reflected my words of wisdom right back at me. "I'm not falling for that, Adelynn Renee. This book is for my eyes only."

"Come on, Mom," she whined. "Why can't I read it?"

"Because I don't want you to."

In the pages of this little book, I'd written the truth about her father, a man she had yet to meet. I didn't feel like taking a trip down memory lane to visit him tonight with her in tow. It would only raise questions that were better left for after she graduated high school—or maybe college. That asshole of a sperm donor didn't deserve her love and affection before she was able to fully understand what had happened a decade ago.

Addy sighed and threw herself on my bed. "I was hoping we could read it together and bond."

Bond? I narrowed my eyes. "You need to stop watching

the Hallmark Channel." I picked up a pair of her pajamas that for some reason were on the floor of *my* bedroom and handed them to her. "Go brush your teeth and climb into bed."

"Ah, Mom."

"Go. Now." I nudged her toward the door. "I'll be in later to kiss you goodnight."

She trudged out the door, her stocking feet sweeping a cluster of dust bunnies with her.

As soon as I heard the bathroom door close, I picked up the diary and popped it open with Addy's paper clip.

Property of Violet Parker

Running my finger over my name, I chewed on my lower lip, remembering. I'd been so young, so clueless. I fanned the pages full of loopy cursive writing. Even my handwriting had been different then—flowing and pretty, not the rushed scrawls I used now.

I stopped on a page with a short, sloppy entry:

July 13th: *Crappity crap! I just realized I totally missed my period. It must be the new birth control pills messing with my system. Seems like the nurse said something about this happening. Maybe I should call the doctor.*

Ha! If only it had just been the pills making my period a no-show. I'd forgotten all about calling the doctor thanks to the full load of college classes I was taking, my full-time job, and, of course, my preoccupation with Addy's father. His blonde hair, golden brown eyes, and hard body had melted my underwear along with my resistance every time he came around to charm me into bed. I'd had a thing for sexy brainiacs back then, especially a science major who talked like Captain James Tiberius Kirk during sex. Don't … stop …Violet.

I flipped a couple of pages, grimacing at the big, bold

strokes I'd used on one of them.

July 29th: *I'm going to kill her!!! How could she? She knows how much I like him. I hate her. I fucking hate her. I CAN'T BELIEVE SHE SLEPT WITH HIM!!!!*

Ah, yes. My little sister, a.k.a. Psycho Susan. I should have known that she was going to be a permanent burr in my ass back when she was four and she cut the hair off all of my Barbie dolls because I'd told her she couldn't play with them while I was at school. Since birth, she'd lived by the motto: What was hers was hers, and what was mine was hers to destroy.

The night I came home early from work and walked in on her naked and gasping in my bed underneath Addy's father was the night I had shut them both out of my life. I still felt a slight kick in my solar plexus whenever the image of them together popped into my head. Her game had sunk to a new level. It was no longer about whom Daddy loved more.

Shaking my head, I flipped forward a few more pages. The writing was short and sweet and slightly smudged.

August 24th: *I'm ten weeks pregnant. Shit!*

I shook my head, remembering the choking fear squeezing my esophagus when I'd stared at the ultrasound image on the monitor. A baby. Oh, my God, a baby.

My sister had still been hot and heavy with Addy's father at the time. We'd become our own soap opera: The Young and the Pregnant. There had been so much drama in the air that summer, especially the night Addy's dad had come to my door and declared his love for me. When I asked why he was having sex with my sister, he claimed it was only because he couldn't have me.

I tried to break his nose with the door when I slammed it, but he'd been too quick for me.

For the next few weeks, I'd chewed my knuckles about whether to tell him or not about the baby. Maybe he really did love me. Maybe, somehow, we could carve a happy family life out of this mess. Maybe I was delusional from pregnancy hormones.

In the end, Natalie, my best friend, had talked me into giving him a chance to be a father.

I turned the pages until I found the entry about me coming clean with him. Two pages later, I had written down his response.

> **September 12th:** *Psycho Susan called me this morning crying hysterically. When she finally calmed down enough to make sense, two words rang clear. "He's gone." So much for having a loving, responsible father for my child. If I ever see the dickhead again, I'm going to tear his nuts off and turn him into a eunuch.*

After our little chat about me bearing his child, the jerk never did contact me to tell me I was going to have to fly solo. Apparently, being a genius didn't guarantee he was smart.

A bunch of self-pity filled the next chunk of pages. Then I came across an entry I remembered all too well.

> **October 5th:** *TWINS! I'm having twins. Oh! My! God! I'm so screwed. The nurse gave me some information on adoption today after I mentioned that the father had run for the hills, abandoning me to raise two babies on my own. The flyer says that they screen the potential parents, including an FBI background check. I don't know what to do.*

I scanned through the next bunch of pages, chuckling at my attempts to return to the dating circuit with a very obvious bump sticking out the front of me. It had been Natalie's idea for me to get out, meet some new men, sniff out a potential father. The only thing I smelled in the dates was a lot of cologne and freakiness.

First, there was the fellow classmate who'd been shocked to learn I was pregnant—he'd just thought I was chubby because I ate like a 300-pound construction worker.

I still wince about the insurance salesman, who after learning why my belly stuck out so far had wanted to cover my baby bump with olive oil and rub his stubble-covered cheeks all over it. Before I shut my apartment door in his face for good, he tried to sell me whole life insurance.

Next came the serious college professor who looked like Magnum P.I. He turned out to be hiding his true age behind dyed hair, a glued-on moustache, and a fake tan. His gray chest hair gave him away, and his desperate fantasy to "bonk" a young female student went unfulfilled by me. My bonking days were long over.

Then there was the angry dentist, the possessed baker, and the narcissistic toy airplane maker. My life had turned into a disturbing nursery rhyme.

Around that time, I finally gave up on men and focused on my new job—Administrative Assistant at a local engineering firm. I decided to keep the babies, much to my family's relief. Well, except for Psycho Susan, who suddenly found the spotlight shining on me and didn't like it that I had toys she couldn't take and mess up—they were attached by umbilical cords.

December 23rd: *Got fired today, one week before my probationary period was up. When I asked the HR rep what I did wrong, I was informed that my sister was caught making a pass at my boss when she came to visit me yesterday (I'd been at the doctor's for my monthly checkup and Susan knew it). "What kind of pass?" I'd asked, explaining that my sister was a perpetual flirt. The kind involving her sitting on his lap in a dress sans her* *underwear. That was probably an accident, I explained straight-faced. Susan sometimes forgot she wasn't wearing underwear—she never has worn them, claiming an allergy to elastic. The HR rep went on to explain that my boss accidentally had his pants down, too. Yikes! Needless to say, after being told that sisters are usually cut from the same cloth and reminded that I was an unwed mother with no baby-father in sight, I was given a week's severance and asked to pack my things and join my boss at the unemployment office. Susan was at my parents' place when I pulled in the drive. Had I been able to catch her, I might have given her a fat lip. Stupid waddle. She swears he came on to her first, and I think Mom even believes her. Criminy. Who is going to hire an almost 28-week-pregnant mother-to-be? I can't even reach past my belly to the glasses in the kitchen cupboard anymore.*

It turned out that the only place that would hire a 28-week-pregnant woman was a 24-hour gas and carryout store. I'd worked there for a full month before my father pulled me aside and begged me to have mercy on him and quit. The stress caused by thinking of his pregnant daughter all alone in a gas station every night had his blood pressure red-lining. I told him that I had to pay rent. He asked me to consider relocating to his basement. He and my mom had talked and agreed they would support me for the first six months of the kids' lives, and then help with babysitting as I got rolling again. My eyes grew misty even now thinking about that conversation with him.

Teary-eyed, I'd told him I'd think about it, which I did three nights later after a red-eyed freak came into the gas station and asked if I needed a foot rub. When I turned him down, he asked if I'd rather practice making another baby. I quit the next morning. My brother moved me back home the following weekend before heading off to the Gobi desert—his next photojournalist gig.

I'd written a lot in my diary during my unemployment. I scanned through lines filled with deep thoughts about the kids, my life, and my aching feet and back. I also plotted revenge schemes, like making a voodoo doll that looked like the sperm donor and backing over it with my car or shaving Susan's head while she slept.

Susan and I had managed to be civil during family dinners, but I stayed in my basement hideout whenever she came to visit the folks. Mom knew better than to ask me to be the bigger person. I was bigger. I was huge, in fact. But there was no way I could get past the crap Susan had pulled.

As Valentine's Day neared, the thoughts in my diary grew darker, full of worries and anxieties over the two little watermelons that would soon need to be pushed out through a rather small opening in my body. I remember wondering what man would ever want me and my deflated body after the babies had come. Short of rubbing bacon all over my pulse points and wearing barbecued pork-rib earrings, I figured I'd be spending the rest of my life sans men.

> **February 9th:** *Cool! I found this small box waiting for me at the table this morning with a card that had my name and a smiley face on it. Inside of the box was a necklace with a daisy pendant. The petals are made of little diamonds and the yellow center is a piece of amber or a yellow sapphire. It looks vintage. I'll have to show it to Aunt Zoe; she's going to love it. She digs this kind of jewelry. Oh, and it came with a matching ring—bonus! Mom and Dad are the best parents ever!*

It turned out they were as surprised as I was by the necklace and ring. I asked all around, but the gift giver remained anonymous, everyone in denial. That should have been my first clue. I blame the pregnancy hormones for my stupidity.

I turned the page, knowing what came next, but caught up in the past anyway.

> **February 14th:** *Guess where I spent the night, diary? In jail. Happy Valentine's Day to me. That's right, eight months pregnant, and there I sat in a damned jail cell. Granted it was only for a half hour before Mom bailed me out, but still—jail. Why, you ask, my dear diary? Because of my PSYCHO SISTER! What started out with me getting pulled over in my parents' pickup for a taillight being out, turned into the truck being listed as stolen, which then became a VIN record check showing over a thousand dollars-worth of unpaid parking tickets and fines. To top it off, while I sat at the police station trying to convince them that I had nothing to do with any of this, one of the officers noticed my pretty new necklace and ring and showed me a photo of the very same pieces—reported stolen. Strike three. I went to jail. A half hour later, my mother dragged my sister into the station. She confessed to having reported my parents' truck stolen seven months ago while she was borrowing it for a few weeks. One of her druggy ex-boyfriends had taken off with the truck for days and racked up all kinds of tickets on it. As for the jewelry, they were hand-me-down gifts from her as a way of apologizing for making me lose my job. She'd scored them from another loser boyfriend who'd ripped off a jewelry store weeks ago and bought her affection with them and other sparkly gifts.*

That had been the last entry I'd made in the diary before I had my twins, the last entry period. That night, I'd gotten into a huge fight with Susan. I told her to never come near me again, and then I spilled the beans about something that still makes shame warm my cheeks.

With my stress level through the roof, I'd gone into labor—a month early. Hours later, the doctor pulled Addy out first and then Layne minutes later. I could still hear their teeny, tiny screeches.

Actually, I could hear them now as they fought with each other from opposite sides of the bathroom door.

"Addy!" I yelled loud enough for the tourists down on Deadwood's historic Main Street to hear me. "Let him in to brush his teeth, dang it!"

I looked back at the diary, touching the picture I'd glued onto the page of both of them snuggled together in the little plastic heating bed. I flipped the page and straightened the wrinkled corner of a picture of Natalie—who'd held my hand through it all—snuggling both babies at once, her face split in a huge grin. The next page had a shot of Aunt Zoe leaning over me while I held my babies. She'd stayed with me in the room until I was cleared to go home and promised me that she'd always have room in Deadwood for all of us if we ever wanted to stay with her.

The poor woman, she probably rued that day now that we'd taken over her home.

"Mom?" Addy hollered, the sound of her footsteps coming toward my room.

I closed and locked the book, shoving it under my mattress for safekeeping before she stepped through the doorway.

"What do you need, Addy?"

She came in and sat on the bed next to me. "I've been wondering something."

"What's that?" I pulled her toward me, tucking her against my side. She smelled like bubble gum flavored toothpaste.

"How old were you when you wrote in that diary?"

"In my twenties."

"Am I in there?"

"Yeah, at the end."

"How come I can't read it?"

I decided to be honest. "Because it takes place during a time in my life when I did something I'm not really proud of."

"You mean getting pregnant with me and Layne?"

"No, Sweetie. It's not that. I'm very proud of you two." When she just stared at me with her golden brown eyes, so like her father's, I explained. "I haven't always been as nice as I am now."

"When are you nice?" I poked her in the ribs, making her giggle. When she sobered, she asked, "Were you mean to someone?"

"Yes. Your Aunt Susan."

"What happened?"

"I made her cry."

"How?"

By telling her the family secret—that Dad would never love her like he loved me because she wasn't really his daughter.

"I said something hurtful to her that I can never take back."

"Is that why you two don't ever talk?"

It's part of the reason. "Yes."

Addy was quiet for a moment. "Do you think you'll ever love someone besides my dad?"

I never loved the jerk, but I didn't mention that. "I already have—you and your brother."

"What if my dad came back around and wanted to spend the rest of his life with you? With us?"

I'd probably end up at the Deadwood police station charged with assault and battery. "That's not going to happen, Addy."

She sighed. "Do you think I'll ever find someone to spend my life with?"

"Well, there's Layne."

"He smells."

"And Elvis." Long live the King—or queen in this case.

"Mom, she's a chicken."

"And me."

"Yeah, but you're a smelly chicken." She giggled again. "Will you let me read your diary someday?"

"Yeah, someday."

"Coolio." She hopped off the bed and slid in her stocking feet over to the door. "Elvis is lonely when I'm not home with her. Can we get a pet pig to keep her company?"

The End ... for now

Interview of Violet Parker

Following is an interview I had with Violet Parker before I began writing *Nearly Departed in Deadwood*. Sometimes I interview several of my characters, sometimes just one. For this book, since I was going to be solely in Violet's head, I only interviewed her.

Enjoy,
Ann

*****

Tin Cup Café in Deadwood, SD

The morning sunshine has just crested the tree-covered hills overlooking Main Street, lighting the red brick road in an orange glow, creeping through the coffee shop's front door. The air drifting through the open door still holds a breath of coolness, the sun's rays haven't heated the sidewalk to a boil yet. From the radio perched on the shelf over the bottles of flavored coffee syrups, Eric Clapton is singing Willie and the Hand Jive on the local station.

The smell of steamed coffee beans makes my mouth water. Unfortunately, they don't have any soy milk on hand, so I'm shit-out-of-luck when it comes to a flavored latte. A big, burly axe-swinging type of a guy lumbers by me on the way to the counter, the century-old, scuffed wood floor creaks under his feet. In his wake, my Diet Coke can wobbles on the small, round table where I sit waiting for Violet Parker to join me.

I shift on the hard, wrought iron seat again, sip some soda pop, and check my cell phone for the time—Violet is fifteen minutes late. She wanted to be at the office by 9 a.m, so our scheduled meeting time of 8 a.m. *should have* given us just enough time to get acquainted.

I glance out the window. Not many tourists line the sidewalks yet, mostly retirees who are up early to gamble away some of their pensions and fast-walking, uniformed folk obviously on their way to work. The espresso maker steams loudly, hissing over Clapton's swanky tale about Way-Out Willie.

A curly-haired blonde appears in the doorway, pausing to scan the room. I recognize Violet's face from her picture on Calamity Jane Realty's website and wave at her. Her tight smile and wrinkled brow show a mixture of frustration and tension as she approaches. Then I notice the child-sized blue handprint on the shoulder of her pale pink blouse and I can't help but chuckle.

Me: Is that paint?

Violet: (She drops into the chair opposite of me.) Is what paint?

Me: The blue handprint on your shoulder.

Violet: (She looks down at her shoulder and the furrows in her brow deepen.) Oh, shit (she says under her breath as she brushes at the blue print, which merely spreads further across her shoulder). Nope, it's chalk, compliments of my son.

Me: Let me buy you a coffee.

Violet: (*Still smudging the chalk around on her shoulder*) I would love a caramel latte, but you don't have to buy it for me.

Me: I owe you one for letting me interview you. I'll be right back. (By the time I return to the table with her steaming latte, she's given up on the blue smudge and is holding her cell phone up in the air.) Here you go (I set it down in front of her).

Violet: I need a new provider. (*She snaps her phone closed.*) What good is a Realtor whose phone gets a signal only when she's standing on top of Terry Peak?

Me: How's the realty business treating you these days?

Violet: (*Her grin twists at the corners.*) I'd be better off selling encyclopedias. Thanks for the coffee (*she sips from the steaming cup*).

Me: How many houses have you sold so far?

Violet: A big, fat zero.

Me: How long have you been working for Calamity Jane Realty?

Violet: Two and a half months. And in that time, I haven't had a single bite. I've shown a handful of clients a vacation house or two, but nobody has signed any offer letters. And if I don't land a deal soon, I'm going to be out on my ass.

Me: What do you mean?

Violet: Jane, the owner, took me on as a favor to my Aunt Zoe with the deal that I had to make a sale within the first three months or she'd have to let me go. She can't afford to carry me if I'm not bringing in any money.

Me: What will you do if she lets you go?

Violet: I don't know. I could try to get my old job back, but I don't want to work with those jerks at the car dealership any more. And I hate being tied to that place for five days a week, plus every other weekend. Being a Realtor has been so much more freeing. I can have lunch with my kids in the park, or take them to doctor's appointments in the middle of the day. They seem so much happier since we moved out of Rapid City.

Me: You're living with your Aunt currently, right?

Violet: Unfortunately.

Me: Don't you get along with her?

Violet: Oh, yes, Aunt Zoe is wonderful. She's happy to share her house with me and the kids—at least that's what she keeps telling me. It's just that I hate mooching off her so much. She lets us stay in her house for free. She won't even take money for a portion of the bills. The most I can do to repay her is keep the cupboards full, which is getting harder and harder with Layne's ever growing stomach.

Me: Is Zoe retired?

Violet: No, she owns and runs the art gallery just up the street. She creates her own glass designs and sells them for an insanely cheap price. She could get four times as much if she wanted, but she insists that her art is for the average American pocketbook. She says there is more money in selling to the masses than the elite, especially in Deadwood, although she does have this deal going right now with an art gallery in Denver. The gallery's owner visited Deadwood last year and stopped in at Zoe's place. He was so impressed with her work that he wants to display and sell her stuff in his gallery. She's hard pressed right now to finish the last four pieces of the twenty he requested by the end of this month.

Me: I'll have to go check out her gallery while I'm in town. So, tell me about your kids.

Violet: (She smiles and grabs her purse, pulling a couple of pictures from her wallet.) This is Adelynn—but she insists on being called Addy. (She shows me a picture of an adorable little blonde holding up what looks like a long, green ribbon toward the camera.)

Me: She likes ribbons?

Violet: Ribbons? (*She looks down at the picture.*) Oh no, that's a dead snake.

Me: Eww.

Violet: Yeah, I know. She's really into animals—alive and dead. She wants to be a veterinarian when she grows up. Aunt Zoe thinks Addy should be a taxidermist since she has no problem handling dead things. (*She holds another picture out.*) And this is Layne, Addy's twin brother.

Me: Twins, huh? (I stare down at the picture of another cute face surrounded by dark blond hair. The boy has Violet's hazel eyes.)

Violet: Yep, born a few minutes apart. Addy came first, so she considers herself Layne's "older" sister. She takes care of Layne, from picking out his clothes some days to making his lunch for school every morning. Not that Layne likes her choice in clothes or healthy foods.

Me: And what does Layne like to do when he's not in school?

Violet: (*She stuffs the pictures back into her purse.*) This summer, he's learning Spanish with Mona.

Me: Really?

Violet: Yes. He wants to be an archeologist, and he's set his sights on South America.

Me: Wow. How old is he?

Violet: They both turned nine last month.

Me: That's ambitious for a nine year old.

Violet: He's watched *Raiders of the Lost Ark* too many times. My dad loves that movie. He and Layne watch one of the three movies from the Indiana Jones series every time they're together.

Me: Who is Mona?

Violet: She's another Realtor at the office. She wants to retire in Mexico in a few years—her sister lives down there and runs a property management company for vacation homes on the beach. Mona bought some learn-Spanish software, and she and Layne are practicing together. She adores my kids, the crazy woman.

Me: Where do your parents live?

Violet: Down in Rapid City.

Me: Was it hard to move away from them?

Violet: Not really. My mom has been pressuring me to date a guy from the neighborhood for the last year. He's about seven years older than me and is pretty good looking, but he's about as exciting as a snail race. Mom often had Ed "joining us" for dinner. I actually folded to Mom's will this last winter and went on a date with Ed. Biggest mistake I could have made. Mom started talking about wedding dresses and reception halls. I could feel the world closing in around me. That's when I saw a billboard for a Realtor school and decided to get out of the rut I'd been spinning my tires in and take a chance on something new and exciting. The kids were game in spite of having to leave their school and friends behind. They have always loved visiting Aunt Zoe and the idea of living up here in the hills seemed pretty romantic to them.

Me: And here you are.

Violet: Yep, here we are. (*She swallowed a gulp of coffee, and then* *her lips curled into a smirk.*) And if I don't make a sale in the next couple of weeks, we'll be on our way up shit creek.

Me: Do you like working at Calamity Jane Realty?

Violet: For the most part. Mona is great and Jane is nice. But then there's Ray …

Me: What's wrong with Ray?

Violet: If there was an award for the World's Biggest Horse's Ass, Ray's walls would be lined with first-place plaques. He's an egotist drowning in "old-boy" mentality, and he has it in for me.

Me: Why?

Violet: Because his nephew is going to school to be a Realtor and Ray wanted him to get the job that Jane gave to me. He is counting the days until the end of the month and the end of my job.

Me: Sounds like a fun guy to work with.

Violet: One week with him and you'd be ready to stab a number 2 pencil in his eye and pray he dies a slow death from lead—well, graphite—poisoning. Natalie wants me to spike his coffee with arsenic, but I don't know where I can buy arsenic these days.

Me: Who's Natalie?

Violet: She's a good friend of mine. She grew up here in Deadwood. I'd hang out with her every summer when I came to stay with Aunt Zoe for a month or so while I was growing up.

Me: What does Natalie do?

Violet: Natalie does a lot of things—she's a dabbler. She dabbles in photography, carpentry, astrology, and the male sex. For money, she is the caretaker for a private campground and lodge just outside of town. She's a jack-of-all-trades.

Me: Sounds like someone else I know named Claire Morgan—especially the campground caretaking bit.

Violet: I know a girl named Claire Morgan. She's Natalie's cousin. Her family lives next to my parent's place. She was in the grade below me. I played kick-the-can with Claire and her younger sister, Kate, all of the time. (She chuckles and swallows the last of her coffee.) Their older sister, Veronica, always insisted we wear reflective vests when we played. How are you supposed to sneak up and kick the can when you stand out like a freaking runway beacon?

Me: Yep, that's Claire and her sisters. It's a small world.

Violet: Especially in the Black Hills. Do you have the time?

Me: (I look down at my cell phone.) It's eight-forty.

Violet: (She grabs her purse and stands.) I'm sorry to cut this short, but I should head to the office. I want to get in before Ray brews a pot of coffee this morning.

Me: You found a place that sells arsenic?

Violet: (She winks.) Something like that. Thanks for the latte.

Me: You're welcome.

Violet: (She pauses at the door and smiles back at me.) Don't be a stranger.

Me: Oh, I won't.

Candy Lover

A Very Short Story from the Ann Charles Vault

I want a lover," Candy announced.

Larry nearly choked on his corndog.

Candy pushed a strand of ash-blonde hair out of her face and tipped her head to the side, her expression thoughtful. "Someone who will accept me for who I am."

She stared across the midway at an old man leading his wife toward the grand stand and sighed. The hot afternoon sunlight reflected off the pool half-full of floating rubber ducks next to her balloon-dart carnival booth, the rays shimmering on her smooth, tan cheeks.

Larry wiped the back of his hand across his mouth and frowned at Candy. "You're pregnant."

Candy grinned at him. "Only seven months."

Adjusting the straps of her dark pink sundress, she focused on the two teenagers who'd stepped up to her counter. Their fingers were entwined, their gazes starry, as if cupid had just knocked their heads together. Candy handed the boy three darts.

A drop of sweat rolled down the middle of Larry's back as he watched the kid throw the first dart. Moving up next to Candy, Larry reached for her as she wavered on her feet. He needed to buy a couple of fans for her. The summer heat roiling off the blacktop couldn't be good for her or the baby.

He helped her sit on the stool next to the helium tank. "Sweetheart, you're so pregnant you can't even see your own shoelaces," he said for her ears only.

Pop! Pop! Pop! The kid nailed three balloons.

"Winner winner, chicken dinner!" Candy called out.

The kid's girlfriend squealed and clapped, pointing at the green stuffed frog hanging on the wall.

Candy used Larry's shoulder to push herself up on her feet again. "Yeah, but some men find pregnant women attractive, don't they?" she asked, grabbing a broom handle with a hook at the end. The frog fell after two nudges. Larry bent down and picked up the frog for her. She took it and handed it to the young girl, watching with an almost wistful smile as the kids walked away, arms around each other, hands in each other's back pockets.

When Larry moved to her side, she looked up at him and asked again, "Don't they, Larry?"

Larry shifted under the weight of her gaze. The gold flecks circling her brown irises seemed to sparkle in the sunlight, mesmerizing him. The heat roiling from the blacktop in front of her booth knocked him back a step. He pulled a rag from his pants pocket and wiped the sweat off his neck.

Across the way, a group of young boys eyed his fake rifles. Maybe it was time to return to his shooting range booth. "I s'pose some do, Candy."

"Then how hard can it be for me to find a lover?"

Grimacing, Larry said, "Why now? Why can't you wait for a couple of more months?"

"Months?" Candy laughed and nudged him with her hip. The smell of her raspberry-scented shampoo mixed with the sweet aroma of Candy made him gulp.

"Come on, Larry," she said, rubbing her hand over her round stomach. Her eyelashes looked white-blonde in the sunlight. "Do you think that just because I'm pregnant I don't want to have sex? That I don't miss being in a man's arms, waking up next to someone, being touched and stroked until I howl at the moon? I may be pregnant, but

I'm not dead."

Touched and stroked ... Damn, he didn't want to think about Candy and sex in the same sentence—not about kissing the smooth, silky skin stretched across her swollen stomach; and definitely not about touching her full, round breasts that were cresting the top of her sundress. He needed to get away from her before he did something stupid that fucked up their friendship.

"Listen, Candy, your sex life is none of my business, but I don't think it would be good for your bab—"

"Never mind, Larry," Candy cut him off and turned her back on him. She waddled over to the helium tank and pulled a balloon out of her pocket.

Larry shrugged, hopped over her counter, and cut through the crowd to his booth.

"Damned woman," he muttered and hurdled his own counter.

He'd known Candy for four months now. He'd watched her blossom from a slender, cute girl into a lush, curvy woman. The asshole who'd knocked her up had been a carnie, too, but he'd left the company before Larry had signed on. What kind of a piece of shit would leave Candy and their baby all alone and never even look back?

Larry had kept to himself the first few weeks on the job, pretending not to notice Candy's tears that fell only when she thought nobody was watching. But then one evening the soft tinkling sound of her laugh had drawn him across the walkway to see what had her so tickled. Later that evening, long after he'd felt the baby moving under her skin, she'd asked him to sit with her outside of her camper and watch the meteor shower. He'd surprised himself by agreeing.

The next week, she'd come over to his counter carrying an elephant ear and split it with him, wiping the powdered sugar off his beard stubble when they finished.

The week after that, he'd offered to drive her to her doctor's appointments. She'd insisted on cooking him breakfast in return as payment. No mortal man could resist her homemade blueberry pancakes, especially when served with her double dimpled-smile.

The sun slipped behind a cloud and Larry glanced over at Candy's booth. His gaze locked on a slick-dressed, leather vested hotshot with greased-back hair leaning on Candy's counter. Whatever the shithead was saying had those dimples showing.

Bile burned his throat. What was wrong with her, flirting so obviously, so wantonly? Where was her pride? He kicked at the shotgun closest to him and knocked it off its holder.

Larry turned away from the two of them. Like he'd said before, Candy's sex life wasn't his business, nor did he have time to watch out for her if she was going to pursue this finding-a-lover bullshit. Besides, he had a booth to run for the next few months until the season ended. After that, he had to fly home to reality, where the day-to-day stress of running his family's construction company made him pop antacids like Tic-Tacs.

Why should he care who she screws?

He pulled his emergency half-empty pack of cigarettes from the shelf under the counter and tapped one into his hand. He'd quit smoking when he'd tagged his brother to take his place running the family business and signed on as a traveling carnie. Until today, he hadn't felt the need to light up. He wasn't even sure where he'd left his lighter.

Candy giggled again, the soft sound enticing his glance her way. His gut twisted. The son of a bitch had his lips on her wrist.

Dragging his eyes away, he stared down at the cigarette in his hand. Why did he care so much about who she had sex with? His mind drifted, imagining what it would be like to peel off her sundress one strap at a time, to see the sweat glistening on her ripe body, to touch...

Oh, God, he had to think of something else, like the subcontractors who always came in twenty percent over estimate, or delivery trucks that never showed up on time, and inspectors who wanted something under the table before they'd give their approval.

He paced across his booth and back. The damned woman had to be ten years his junior. He had no business thinking of her as more than the friend she'd become, more than a woman about to bring a child into this world on her own with no man to help.

His gaze snuck back across to where she stood, fanning herself under the sun's rays.

The memory of sitting next to her on her counter weeks ago while sharing a bag of doughnut holes played through his thoughts. She'd smelled like the vanilla milkshake she'd spilled down her mini-dress, her laughter infectious. When she leaned back on her palms and her dress inched up her legs, he'd noticed how the freckles on her thigh formed a "C." The urge to trace the letter and then explore what else she was hiding under her dress had sucked all of his breath from his lungs. He'd launched himself off the counter so fast, he'd practically fallen on his ass at her feet.

Across the way, the asshole tugged Candy down to whisper in her ear, her breasts threatening to fall out of her dress. Her sweet giggle scraped over Larry's nerves.

"No fucking way is this going to happen," he said and threw the cigarette down. Vaulting over his counter, he plowed through the crowd and yanked Candy's arm away from the asshole's grip.

He climbed over her counter and stood in front of her, the rapid rise and fall of his chest had nothing to do with the afternoon heat.

Candy looked up at him, her eyes narrowing. "What are

you doing, Larry?"

"You've found him," he said and pulled her close. Her hard stomach rubbed against his, her shoulders soft and smooth under his palms. Cupping her face, he lowered his mouth to hers, starting off slow, gentle, afraid of hurting her.

But then she wrapped her arms around his neck and kissed him back, frenzied and hard, moaning his name against his lips.

"Candy," he groaned and fed the need that had grown with each passing day he'd watched her blossom, each shared laugh, each brush of her skin against his. Jesus, she tasted so damned sweet.

When he lifted his lips and looked into those golden-lashed eyes, Candy grinned up at him. "What took you so damned long?"

GOLDWASH

Shorts

The Old Man's Back in Town

AUTHOR NOTE: This short story is a bit of a puzzle. Each scene is a different variation of the same story for a reason, which you'll learn at the end. See if you can pick up on the clues along the way and figure out the puzzle before you finish the story. Thank you for giving it a try! —Ann

Goldwash, Nevada
December 24th

Jingle bells, jingle bells, jingle all the way. Oh what fun it
is to ride in a one horse open sleigh.

W̶ould you turn off that Christmas crap and help me clean
up all this blood?" I said, throwing a wet rag at my cousin
Buffalo as he nursed a mug of beer at the end of the bar.

Buffalo dodged the rag. "Jeez, Montana, can't you let a
man enjoy a nostalgic moment? Where's your holiday
spirit?"

"I think I flushed it the other night after you came by

bearing green and red M&Ms and spiked eggnog." I dragged the bucket of sudsy water over to the pool of blood, pulling the stools out on each side of Buffalo.

Damn, there was a lot of blood.

The ammonia in my mop water smelled almost clinical, reminding me of a hospital room, blocking out the coppery tang as the red mop-head creaked and swooshed.

He chuckled. "Girl, you really need to find some new friends."

"And family." I poked him in the ribs, making him grunt mid-drink. "I'm closing the bar early tonight. You can either help me with this mess or drag your sorry ass home to that pitifully fat bulldog of yours."

"Leave Brunhilda out of this." Buffalo wiped the beer foam moustache from his upper lip with the sleeve of his brown thermal shirt. "So, how did all of this blood get here, anyway?"

I paused, replaying the night's events. Things had been a little hectic with the drunken caroling and smooching under the mistletoe, making everything jumble together in my memory. Since The Ugly Rooster was the only watering hole in over a fifty-mile radius, the annual holiday party lured in the wild life from the nearby ranges and basins in droves.

"I can't remember. It just kind of appeared." Yet cleaning it up felt like momentary déjà vu.

"How can you not remember this much blood? You must be getting daft from old age."

Sure, all of my thirty-six old years. "You have two years on me, remember?"

"Yeah, but unlike you, I'm getting wiser."

"Wiser? Weren't you the one who broke your arm earlier this year wrestling with your neighbor's pig?"

"There's a rational explanation for that."

I grinned, "Yeah, but you lost the bet, and then your

girlfriend left you for the winner."

"That woman was nuttier than a squirrel turd. Her leaving was my good fortune."

I couldn't have agreed more, especially after hearing she'd knocked Buffalo out cold with a cast iron skillet during one of her drunken fits.

"It just confirmed what I'd told you all along," he continued. "She wasn't the 'one' for me."

"Right. I suppose you're sticking with Brunhilda being your one-and-only still?"

"Well, she is the prettiest girl in this dusty pit stop. Except for you, of course, but kissin' my cousin doesn't pop my pup-tent."

"Thank the Maker for that. Now help me clean up this blood or get the hell out of my bar."

Buffalo hopped off his seat and started wiping down the legs of the stools. "What has you so ornery lately, Monty?" he asked. "You used to dig the holidays, putting up little trees all over in here, decorating the old joint with colored lights. Ever since Joel left for Vegas, you—"

I stopped mopping mid-swish. "This has nothing to do with that son of a bitch."

"Right. I see you're still 'over him' almost four months later."

"If only I had the power to turn men into dung beetles."

"Joel always could charm the skin off a snake."

With just a wink and a grin that bastard certainly had made me rise up and dance a good too many times to count.

Leaning on the mop, I frowned down at the wet, scarred up wooden floor. "Honestly, it's not Joel that has me feeling pissy. I have a gut feeling that something isn't quite right out there tonight."

"It's just the wind. You never did like it when it howled.

Remember when you were a little pissant and you'd hide under the bed during sand storms? Your mom would have to lure you out with Snickerdoodles."

My eyes watered for a split-second, remembering my momma and her sweet, coaxing smile. It had been her idea to name me Montana, after her home state. Momma had said my big blue peepers had reminded her of Big Sky country as soon as I shot out of the womb and blinked them open.

"Yeah, maybe it's just the wind," I said. "But I'd feel safer at home."

"Is this about those calls you've been getting with all that heavy breathing?"

Maybe. "Nah, that's just some stupid kid screwing around."

"I still think you should tell the sheriff about them. If not the calls, then at least he needs to know about all of this blood."

"Enough about the blood. It's all gone." I dipped the mop-head in the red water. "All the sheriff will do is tell me to file a report and change my number. The calls will go away if I just keep ignoring them."

"Fine, don't listen to me, like usual." He leaned against the bar, watching me rinse the mop-head. "So what makes you think you're safer alone at home?"

"My 12-gauge."

He laughed. "You want me to bring my forty-five over to spend Christmas with your shotgun?"

"Thanks." I squeezed his shoulder. "But I'm not good company tonight. Too many memories. I need to re-align my chakras or some crap like that."

"Have you been reading those books full of motivational mumbo-jumbo again?"

I shook my head. "Somebody keeps carving quotes on my bathroom stall doors."

The bell over the door jingled.

"Bar's closed," I hollered.

"Even for an old friend?" The deep voice raised the hairs on the back of my neck.

I turned slowly, gripping the mop handle to keep from falling over.

"Well, well, well," Buffalo said. "Look what Santa brought you, Monty, a hunka-hunka burnin' heartache. You must have been naughty this year."

Joel Andersen closed the door, silencing the wail of a Nevada winter gale.

My eyes narrowed as Joel strolled closer. His black hair was ruffled from the wind, his chin covered with dark stubble. The lines bracketing his eyes showed a tension that his big, easy grin couldn't hide.

Of all of the gin joints in all the tumbleweed-choked towns in the world, he strolled into mine. "I said the bar's closed."

"I heard you, Shooter." He used my childhood nickname like he still had a right to, the jerk. He patted Buffalo on the back. "How's the restoration coming along, Buffalo?"

Buffalo was in the process of fixing up the historic Goldwash Grand Hotel. A dilapidated monument of Goldwash's prosperous past, the old brick hotel had been left to decay under the harsh desert sun for over forty years along with the rest of the town after the last of the gold had been hauled away.

"When I'm not tied up in historical committee red tape, it's great. How are those Vegas lights?"

"Twinkling," Joel answered, but his emerald-colored eyes held mine captive, fire burning in their depths like usual when he planned to woo my pants right off of me. "Always twinkling."

My heart shook off a layer of dust and started to pitter-patter, the damned lonely traitor.

There went my plans for a sober Christmas Day.

"What do you want?" I asked, not mincing words.

His gaze trailed down the front of my green T-shirt, old blue jeans, and landed on my red cowboy boots. "I missed you, too, Montana. Got your Miss Claus getup on, I see."

"Go back to Vegas." I dragged the mop bucket across the floor and kicked it into the corner. "You're not welcome 'round here anymore."

And here I'd had the silly notion that I was over the pain of his leaving me. The grinding sensation chewing away in my chest called me on that lie.

"Come on, Shooter. Is that any way to treat a guy just out of the cold on Christmas Eve? Where's your holiday spirit?"

"She flushed it down the toilet," Buffalo said, hooking a stool with his boot for Joel to sit next to him just like old times.

"Can it, Buffalo." I moved behind the bar, pouring myself a shot of whiskey, my trembling hand itching to throw the amber liquor in Joel's face. How dare he just show up on my doorstep after months of silence? Months! He could have at least sent a postcard. Or called to let me know he was still alive.

Hold up. Maybe Joel was the heavy breather who had kept calling me this past week.

I glared at him. "If you're the jackass who's been harassing me on the phone, you can knock that shit off."

His brow wrinkled. "Harassing you how?"

After several seconds of staring him down, I bought into his innocence. "Never mind."

"Have you told the sheriff about it?"

"She refuses to tell your brother," Buffalo answered for me. "She's still more stubborn than smart. That hasn't changed since you left."

"She never has liked change much," Joel said, watching me like I might drop my glass and draw on him. "That's why it took so long to get her to stop thinking of me as just an old friend and go out on a date."

And look what happened when I did. My heart had been flattened like road kill.

That was enough reminiscing for a Christmas Eve. Next they'd want to start singing Bing Crosby and Danny-freaking-Kaye tunes. "You both need to get out of my bar before I fill you full of holes."

"She's bluffing," Buffalo said. "She just told me her shotgun is at home."

"How about one drink for old times' sake?" Joel suggested, leaning his elbows on the bar. His grin said good times, but his eyes warned of something darker.

I slammed back the shot, thunking the glass down on the bar. The whiskey burned a trail all the way to my boot heels. "There. Consider that drink done had. Lock the door on your way out."

Without another word, I pushed through the swinging half-doors that led back to my office where I planned to hide until Joel went back to Vegas and took his heartbreaking eyes with him.

The bastard didn't let me make it that far.

"Montana," Joel said from behind me, his tone no longer full of jest. "I need to talk to you."

"I'm busy," I called over my shoulder without slowing. "Stop back next year sometime."

He caught my arm. "This can't wait."

"Really?" I whirled on him. "After months of dead silence, you suddenly feel chatty? I don't think so. Go home to your fancy Vegas condo and leave me be."

I tugged my arm free, stormed into my office, and tried to slam the door behind me. But his foot screwed up my grand exit, sneaking in between the door and frame, keeping me from locking him out of my office and my life.

He shoved his way inside, closed the door, and leaned against it.

Crossing my arms over my chest, I hit him with a double-barreled glare. "We have nothing left to say to each other, Joel."

"I'm not here because of us."

I took a step back. Damn, that stung. If there was one thing I could always count on from Joel, before and after we'd started having knock-my-boots-off sex, it was his brutal honesty. "Yeah, well, there is no 'us' anyway, so that point is moot."

"You are such a lousy liar," he said, his smirk making a show. "But we'll get to that later."

There wasn't going to be an "us" involved with "later" as far as I was concerned. My heart was still duct taped from last time.

"You've got trouble coming your way," he said, all serious.

"Yeah, I'm looking at it."

"You're going to wish it was just me." His face hardened. "Your ex-husband escaped from prison a week ago."

What! "Are you serious?" He nodded and my knees wobbled. "Oh, shit."

Joel grabbed me as I started to fold, leading me to the old silver couch I used as a bed when I was too tired—or drunk—to make it home. He kneeled in front of me, pushing my long bangs out of my eyes. He smelled like the desert, all fresh and spicy, yet sweet and earthy—his scent. I wanted to wrap it around me, to roll around in it like a wild horse in a spring meadow, and forget about my ex out from behind bars, free to kill again.

"Who escapes from prison in this day and age?" I asked.

"Ruthless bastards who have connections on the

outside."

"So, that's why you're here, *Detective* Andersen. The Las Vegas Police Department has you working overtime on Christmas Eve?" It had nothing to do with me, the woman he'd left behind for a job in the big city, rather with an escaped convict he was hunting down.

"Yes."

Brutally honest Joel. He ran true, had to give him that.

I dropped my focus to my hands, which were all pretzel-twisted together. "Well, I haven't seen him."

"Good, but you're probably on his list of must-sees this holiday season."

"Does your brother know about this?"

He nodded. "He was supposed to have one of his deputies sitting outside your bar tonight."

"It's Christmas Eve, Joel. A time for families, not babysitting the local bar owner. But that explains why your brother stopped by earlier at lunch and suggested that I cancel tonight's holiday shindig."

"Why didn't you?"

"I couldn't. It's a Goldwash tradition. Besides, too many locals need it to make it through the holidays."

"You realize he may try to kill you again."

"He can try."

"Listen—"

"But I might kill him first."

Joel pushed to his feet, pacing in front of me. "Montana, think about what you're up against. He's twice your size, built up with years of prison bulk and revenge, and probably pissed as hell at the woman who helped put him behind bars."

This explained the anxiety I'd been feeling in my gut for the last couple of days. The universe had been sending me get-the-hell-out-of-Dodge vibes. I needed to go home, grab my 12-gauge and some supplies, and head for the hills for a few days. Maybe Buffalo could cover for me here over New Year's.

Brushing my hands down my jeans, I shoved to my feet, testing out my shaky knees. They felt solid again. "Thanks for driving out here to let me know. I appreciate the heads-up." I crossed to the door. "Now, you've done your duty, so you're free to head out."

I held open the door for him.

"Stop being so stubborn," he said, grabbing my arm. "I'm not going anywhere tonight."

"Joel," I glared down at his hand on my arm, "you're out of your jurisdiction, especially when it comes to touching me. Or have you forgotten that fact?"

He forced the door shut and walked me backwards until I was up against my desk, his body pressed into mine. "I haven't forgotten a single thing about touching you."

Damn, I'd missed his hard angles.

His long, dark eyelashes lowered, his green eyes full of sins of the flesh. "Did you miss me, Shooter?"

Like rain in Death Valley. "Kiss my ass, Andersen."

"In a heartbeat. Are you wearing a thong or that underwear that only covers half of your cheeks?"

My core temperature hit a molten level. My limbs tingled, wanting to wrap around him and cling. But I stood still, hiding behind a jutted chin. "Stop flirting with me. You lost that right when you walked out."

He trailed his knuckles along my collar bone, teasing. "I asked you to come with me."

I clenched my fists, determined not to lean into him. "No, you informed me that your career was stagnant. That there was nothing left in Goldwash for you, so you were going to try your hand in Vegas."

"Same thing."

I planted both palms on his chest and pushed him back. "Your communication skills have never been your strong point."

He allowed me the extra space, dropping his arms to his sides. "And your stubbornness will be the death of you."

"That's no longer your concern."

"Bullshit, Shooter." His eyes traveled down over my T-shirt. "You look thinner."

Heartache made for a great dieting plan. Damn him for looking better than ever in his flannel shirt.

"I've been a little stressed."

"How's your dad doing on his own?" he asked.

"Coping. He helps out here some nights when the loneliness gets too much." We made quite a pair—lonely and lonelier.

"Working with you can't be easy."

"I'm nicer to him than to you." Dad didn't choose a career over me.

His grin came quick. "I mean because you look so much like your mom when she was younger." He reached out and fingered a strand of my hair. "Especially with your hair the same shade of auburn as hers. I like this longer, wavy cut. Makes you look more bohemian. She'd have approved."

My eyes watered, damn it. I couldn't let him use my momma to soften me up. I blinked away the tears. "What do you want from me, Joel?"

He released my hair. "I've chased you since you wore pigtails, Shooter. Just this once, couldn't you have chased me?"

"I have a bar to run."

"Buffalo could have filled in. Your sister and dad would have helped. Your brother, too."

"It's not their responsibility. Momma left the place to me."

"She didn't expect you to chain yourself to it."

"It's been in our family since this town was founded over a century ago. You don't just walk away from that."

"Excuses."

I growled, pushing away from the desk, needing the room between us to hold my ground. "What was I supposed to do, Joel? Just drop everything in my life to follow you like a puppy, happy for any bits of attention you gave to me?"

"No." His gaze bore into mine, all traces of humor and lust tempered. "You were supposed to ask me not to go."

Huh? That stole the wind from my world, my tumbleweed of frustration rolling to a stop. "And if I had?"

He shrugged. "I would have stayed."

My mouth fell open. "So this was all some big test?"

"No test. I was tired of running in place. It was change."

I threw my hands up. "Well, you got your change, didn't you? Was it as good for you as it was for me?"

He bridged the distance between us in three long strides, catching my hand, tugging me toward him. "A little birdie told me you're going home alone every night."

He had me so discombobulated that I let him pull me into his arms. "Tell your brother to mind his own goddamned business. He doesn't know everything that happens in this town."

"Are you sleeping with someone?"

"Maybe."

"Your pants are on fire."

He tended to have that effect on the lower half of my body. "Joel, you can't just come back here and expect me to fall into your arms."

"Don't fall then." He leaned in close, his lips even closer. "Walk."

I almost danced to his snake charms again. "Stop it." I nudged him aside and yanked open the door, escaping down the hall toward the bar.

"Montana," he called. "Come back to me."

"You need to leave," I yelled back. If he didn't, I might do something stupid and tell him how much I still loved him.

"I'm not leaving without you."

I shoved out into the dark room and was halfway along the front of the bar toward the door before I fully registered that the lights were off—all of them, even the beer lights I usually left on in the windows.

"Buff?" My boot toe connected with what felt like a rolled up carpet on the floor. I stumbled to my knees, my hand coming down in something warm, wet, slippery. "What the hell?"

"Hi, Montana," a scratchy voice said in the darkness. Fear spider-crawled up my spine. "Aren't you going to welcome me home, baby?"

I gasped, my heart hurtling into a full-on panic. My ex was here, waiting for me in the darkness. I shouldn't have left my shotgun at home.

"Sweetheart, I'm serious," Joel said from the swinging doors. "I want you to come with—"

"Joel, watch out!" I yelled. Then a shot rang out over my head.

"No!" Scrambling, I tried to get to my feet and run to Joel, but I slipped on the wet floor.

A volley of gunshots blasted around me as I fell, my shoulder exploding in pain, my head connecting with a stool on the way down. The crack echoed through my skull...

Goldwash, Nevada
December 24th

On the first day of Christmas my
true love gave to me ...

Would you turn off that Christmas crap and help me clean
up all this beer?" I said, throwing a wet rag at my cousin
Buffalo as he nursed his drink at the end of the bar.

Buffalo caught the rag mid-air. "Jeez, Montana, can't
you let a man enjoy a nostalgic moment? Where's your
holiday spirit?"

"I think your dog ate it." I dragged a bucket of sudsy
water over, pulling the stools out on each side of Buffalo,
and mopped up the beer pooled there. The clinical,
ammonia-heavy odor from the mop bucket blocked out any
yeasty whiffs of beer.

"Leave Brunhilda out of this." Buffalo reached down
and scratched his bulldog between her fake reindeer antlers.

"I'd like to, but her fat butt is in my way." I nudged her
with the toe of my red cowboy boot. Brunhilda grunted, but
didn't budge. "I'm not even supposed to have dogs in here.
If the state health inspector were to walk in, I'm screwed."

"Nah. I'd just explain that she's our Aunt Harriet. They
kind of look alike. Besides, if it weren't for me and

Brunhilda, you'd be all alone on Christmas Eve."

Sad, but true. I needed some new friends. "I'm closing the bar early tonight. You can either help me with this mess or drag both of your sorry asses home."

"Just call me Cinderella," Buffalo said, setting his glass to the side. "Whoever spilled all of this good beer should be thrown in the hoosegow."

Something about my standing there with a mop in my hand spurred déjà vu. I tried to remember what had happened earlier in the night, but everything jumbled together in my memory—the two old drunks caroling on top of the bar like they were Vegas night club singers, the feisty retiree in the red velvet running suit bouncing around and dangling mistletoe over her head. It was a wonder someone hadn't broken a hip.

"You have everything you need for New Year's?" Buffalo asked.

"Everything but a date."

"You can be mine—minus anything disgustingly sexual."

I grinned. "The feeling is mutual, Buff. I still can't believe you got in a fight with your girlfriend over your neighbor's pig and ended up with a broken arm."

"I can't believe she came at me with that cast iron skillet." He bent down and scratched Brunhilda's back. "But we're sure glad that crazy bitch left us, aren't we old girl? She was just jealous because you're prettier than she ever was."

"You and that dog are spending way too much time together. Next you'll be telling me she's the 'one' for you."

"You know I don't believe in just having one woman for more than a couple of months. It's unnatural."

"You're unnatural. Now help me clean up this beer or get the hell out of my bar."

Buffalo wiped the bar down in silence for several

seconds. "I wonder what Joel is up to. You'd think he'd come home for the holidays, pay his dad a visit, drop in and share a drink with the latest woman he'd kicked to the curb."

I stopped mopping mid-swish, my hackles rising unbeknownst to Buffalo apparently, because he kept rambling. "The guy always hated staying in the big city too long, said it rotted his lungs."

"Can we not talk about that son of a bitch tonight?" I asked. "I'm hoping to have a sober holiday."

Buffalo shook his head. "I can't believe you're still not over him. I hate to say it after he left you like he did, but that means something, Monty. You should probably go see him, run some tests, and find out if it's really love."

"Or just chronic heartburn," I said, glaring at Buffalo. "If only I had the power to turn men into dung beetles."

He laughed. "You know, it's not your fault. Joel always could charm the spines off a prickly pear cactus if he put his mind to it. I'm just surprised it took him so long to get you into bed."

I'd resisted Joel's wooing as long as humanly possible, but the bastard had convinced me I was special. Not to mention that his pheromones could be a superpower. "He certainly had a talented tongue."

Buffalo cringed. "Hey, come on. There are things about you two that I never want to know."

"You started this."

The phone behind the bar rang.

Looking over at the display screen, Buffalo frowned. "It says, 'unlisted number'."

"Don't answer. It's just going to be a bunch of heavy breathing."

"Did you tell the sheriff about these calls?"

"No."

"You've been getting them for a week now. It's time to

take this seriously, stat."

"Did you just say *stat*?"

He continued, ignoring my interruption. "You need to let the sheriff know about them so you can get it put on file in case you end up shooting someone again."

"That was an accident. How many times do I have to tell you I'm sorry?"

"Every time my scar throbs." He leaned against the bar, watching the mop-head move back and forth. "I sure wish you had that damned shotgun of yours handy."

I winked at him. "What makes you think I don't?"

"That's my girl."

The bell over the door jingled.

"Bar's closed," I hollered.

"Hello, Montana." The deep voice nearly stopped my heart. I turned slowly, squeezing the mop handle in a death grip. "Aren't you going to welcome me home with open arms?"

"Well, well, well," Buffalo said, his tone low. "Look what Santa left behind for you, Monty, some achy-breaky heartachey. You must have been extra naughty this year." He slid me a grin. "I told you to stop talking bad about Aunt Harriet."

I growled in the back of my throat as Joel walked closer, shucking his thick coat. With his ruffled midnight-black hair, stubble-covered square jaw, and emerald green eyes, he looked like sin in the skin, all cock of the walk.

But when he stopped in front of me, I noticed the crows' feet bracketing his eyes, showing a tension that his big, easy grin couldn't hide.

Don't say it's a fine morning or I'll shoot ya, I heard John Wayne say in my head. "I said the bar's closed."

"I heard you, Shooter." His use of my childhood nickname prickled my pucker. He patted Buffalo on the back. "Hey, Buff, you given any thought to my investment offer for the ol' Goldwash Grand?"

Buffalo had recently "retired" after making a shitload of money in software development over in Silicon Valley and was blowing it all on fixing up the local historic hotel, which needed a lot of love and a wad of cash after sitting in the Nevada sun and wind for the last forty years.

"I don't feel right taking money from friends or family."

"Hey!" I gaped at Buffalo. "What about that fifty bucks you still owe me?"

"Well, *your* money feels just fine, Monty."

Buffalo turned back to Joel. "How are those Vegas lights?"

"Too damned bright and crowded," Joel answered Buffalo, but his green eyes held mine captive, fire burning in their depths like usual whenever he tried to sex my boots off. "Not enough big blue sky there."

I curled my toes, holding on to my boots and my heart.

"What do you want, Joel?" I asked, not mincing words.

His gaze hovered on the front of my T-shirt. "I missed you, too, Montana."

The asshole had a lot of nerve, strutting back into my world and throwing hungry looks in my direction.

I let the mop handle fall against the bar and walked around to the wall full of liquor bottles. *Eenie-meenie-minie-moe.* I grabbed a bottle of whiskey, sending him a stink-eyed glance. "Go back to the bright lights, Joel. It took me long enough to scrape you off the bottom of my boots last time you came around."

Buffalo whistled between his teeth. "She ain't pullin' her punches tonight, Joel."

"Come on, Shooter," Joel said. "Is that any way to treat a guy just out of the cold on Christmas Eve? Where's your holiday spirit?"

"Brunhilda ate it," Buffalo said.

Brunhilda swiveled an ear in our direction.

I poured myself a shot, my trembling hand itching to pour the amber liquor over Joel's head. How dare he show his mug in here after kicking me in the teeth the last time we talked?

The phone rang. I glanced at the caller ID—unlisted number again. *Damn it!*

Reaching over, I grabbed the phone base, tore it off the wall, threw it on the floor, and stomped down on it with my heel.

"Breathe all over that, jerkoff," I said and tossed back the shot of whiskey. It burned a path all the way down, slamming into my toes.

With a tight smile for Buffalo, then Joel, I said, "You both need to get out of my bar before I fill you full of holes."

"She ain't bluffing," Buffalo said. "She's got her shotgun with her."

"What's up with the phone, Montana?" Joel asked, leaning his elbows on the bar. His eyes tried to read my face like the wrinkles and sunspots had tall tales to tell.

"None of your business. Lock the door on your way out."

Without another word, I grabbed the bottle of whiskey and shoved through the swinging half-doors that led back to my office.

Change of plans this Christmas Eve—chuck the old Westerns marathon and cuddle up with a bottle of firewater until Joel went back to Vegas and took his heartbreaking grin with him.

The bastard didn't let me make it that far.

"Montana," Joel called from behind me. "I need to talk to you."

"Go to hell." I stepped through my office doorway. "You're killing my holiday buzz."

He followed on my boot heels, shutting the door

behind him. "This can't wait."

"Really?" I whirled on him, whiskey sloshing in my hand. "What's so damned important that you had to break the four months of beautiful silence we had going?"

He took the bottle from me and put it on my desk. "Your ex-husband escaped from prison a week ago."

What! "Are you serious?" At his nod, I stumbled backwards, falling onto the silver couch I used to sleep on in the old days when my parents ran the bar. "Oh, fuck."

Joel kneeled in front of me, holding my clammy hands in his. He smelled fresh from the desert, all spicy and earthy, like the tumbleweed he was. Just last week I was daydreaming about using a nail gun to pin him to a fence once and for all.

"We've had an APB out for him since he disappeared. Yesterday, a convenience store owner down in Beatty recognized him and called the cops, but he slipped by them."

"You're sure it was him?"

"He bought unfiltered cigarettes, black licorice, and orange soda pop."

I grimaced. Yep, that was him all right. "How did he escape from prison in this day and age?"

"His girlfriend seduced a guard."

"It's that simple, huh?"

"There's a bit more to it, but you get the gist."

"So, is that why you're here, *Detective* Andersen? The Las Vegas Police Department has you working overtime on Christmas Eve looking for my ex?"

In other words, I was just part of his *job*—the source of our breakup.

"Yes."

I had never quite gotten used to his brutal honesty, no matter how many times he lashed me with it. I twisted my hands together to keep from giving him a shiner. "Well, I haven't seen him."

"Tell me why you broke the phone."

"Some asthmatic keeps calling me."

"How long has this been going on?"

"About a week now." My eyes widened as a light bulb went on. "It's him, isn't it?"

Joel shrugged. "It's a good bet you're on his list of must-sees this holiday season, and I doubt he plans on doing the dance of the sugar plum fairy with you."

"Does your brother know about this?"

He nodded. "Rick has had one of his deputies sitting outside your bar tonight."

"Nothing like having to babysit the local bar owner on Christmas Eve."

"Why didn't you close like Rick asked?"

"The holiday party is a Goldwash tradition and the only get-together for most of the locals living alone out here. You know that."

"Montana, he's going to try to kill you again." Joel's fingers brushed along my jaw.

I pushed his hand away and stood. "*Try* being the operative word."

"Don't be going off half-cocked." Joel rose to his feet. "Look where that left you last time."

"In bed with you?"

He shot me a crooked grin. "I was talking about jail."

Oh, yeah. I hadn't thought about that in a long time. "Well, maybe I'll kill him first. Have you considered that, Detective?" I paced in front of my desk. "I have several boxes of ammo in my garage. I'll just hole up at home for a few days. Buff will cover for me here."

"Shooter," Joel said, reaching for my arm.

I dodged him. "No, I don't want to take any chances of getting someone hurt. I'll just have to shut the bar down." Which pissed me off after all I'd spent in preparation for the New Year's party.

"Damn it, woman," Joel grabbed me and yanked me against his chest. "Shut up and listen to me for a second."

I blinked up at him. "You're out of your jurisdiction, Joel, especially when it comes to touching me. Or have you forgotten that fact?"

He walked me backwards until I was up against my desk, his body tight against mine. "I haven't forgotten a single thing about touching you, Montana. You're pretty much branded onto my brain."

The heat coming off him melted the layer of frost I'd built up over the last few months. Damn, I'd sure missed his rough edges.

"If this is your attempt to distract me from filling my ex-husband full of lead, it's not gonna work."

"Oh, yeah? I bet I can still give you goosebumps." His long, black eyelashes lowered, his green eyes dark with carnal intent.

"If your brother sent you in here to deter me for some reason …"

"My brother doesn't know I'm here. Nobody does."

"Buffalo does."

"Buff is going home." He ran his lips over my collar bone, making my heart bounce around like a playful foal, the double-crossing muscle.

His tongue flicked over the pulse in my neck. "I want you, Shooter. No matter how much you piss me off with your mule-headedness, I always want you, damn it."

Not exactly a Shakespearean sonnet, but his words made my head rummy anyway.

"I know you feel the same," he whispered against my skin. "It's in those big blue eyes of yours."

I closed my peepers, trying to focus on the many ways I'd wanted to hurt Joel since our last conversation. "Kiss my ass, Andersen."

"Sure thing. Take off your pants." He gripped my hips, lifting me onto the desk, angling between my thighs. "Please tell me you're still on the pill."

I slid my hands along his broad shoulders, retracing the lines and ridges I'd missed. "It doesn't matter. This is not going to happen."

He covered my lips with his, touched his tongue to mine, and all hell broke loose in my chest.

I scooted closer to him, tearing at his shirt buttons. "Stop flirting with me," I said, ripping open the last two buttons, leaning in to smell his skin then taste it. Warm and salty, like the desert hardpan.

I felt his groan vibrate against my mouth. "I missed you, Montana. All of you. Especially your smart mouth."

"Stop talking before you piss me off again."

He chuckled, lifting my chin until my gaze locked with his. "I thought about you day and night. Especially in the shower."

"Oh, yeah? You have a funny way of showing it."

He trailed kisses along my jaw, leaving a line of heat in their wake. "You're the one who refused to come with me when I asked."

Gasping as he nipped my earlobe, I said, "I don't remember you doing any asking, just informing me after you decided."

"I thought the ring said it all."

I tugged his flannel shirt off his arms. "It was a full-sized nose ring straight off a bull."

"I cleaned it first. Besides, it was symbolic—you could lead me around anywhere by it. Buffalo thought it was romantic."

"Maybe you should have given it to him." Joel's thermal undershirt dropped to the floor. "Your communication skills have never been your..." I paused to swallow the excess saliva the sight of his bared skin produced, the dark dusting of hair pointing my eyes southward, "…your strong point."

He tugged my T-shirt over my head. "And your stubbornness will be the death of you, unless I can help it."

"That's no longer your concern."

"You and I both know that's not true." His fingers traced along the lace at the top of my bra, making me squirm. He leaned down and kissed the swell of skin just above the fabric. "You look thinner, sweetheart."

"I've been busy," I lied.

His gaze held mine, suddenly serious. "Tell me there's nobody else in the picture."

There never would be, but I had to salvage my pride, what little of it he hadn't stripped from me yet again tonight. "Why didn't you call me back, Joel?"

He cupped my face, brushing his lips over mine so slowly, so tenderly, like he wanted to savor them. I couldn't hold in the moan that reached up from my heart.

"I've chased you since you wore pigtails, Shooter," he whispered. "Just this once, couldn't you have chased me?"

"You ran too far."

His mouth trailed down my neck. "I wouldn't have run anywhere if you'd told me you wanted me to stay."

I leaned back on the desk, tipping my head back to give him more access, wanting to ask if that meant what I thought it did, but the sound of glass breaking crashed through my lust-filled haze. I froze. "Did you hear that?"

"Hear what?"

Another crash resounded. *Buffalo!*

"That." I shoved him back, scooped up my T-shirt from the floor, and raced out the door, pulling the shirt over my head as I ran.

"Montana," he said from the doorway. "Come back to me."

I shoved out the swinging doors into the darkness and

was halfway along the front of the bar when I realized the lights were off—all of them, even the beer lights I usually left on in the windows.

"Buffalo?" I said. My boot toe connected with what felt like a body, making me stumble to my knees, my hand coming down on something warm, wet, slippery.

A heavy, coppery scent filled my head.

"Oh, God. Buffalo?" I reached for his body, but it wasn't there, just blood, pooled all around me.

Then I heard it, the breathing in the darkness.

"Hey, baby," an all-too familiar scratchy voice said.

I froze, my heart throwing itself against my rib cage like it wanted to bust free and high-tail it out of town. Maybe if I just held still in the blackness, he wouldn't see me.

"Aren't you going to welcome me home?"

"Montana," Joel said from the direction of the swinging doors. "Are you okay?"

I heard the click of a hammer being cocked back.

"Joel, get down!" I yelled.

A shot rang out over my head.

"No!" I screamed, struggling to my feet, lurching toward where Joel stood by the swinging doors. Only he wasn't there.

A second shot exploded. Then a third, which tore across the outside of my shoulder, stinging like a son of a bitch.

I slipped, the blood slick as ice under my boots. On the way down, my skull connected with something hard. Pain flared above my left ear and ripped through my skull...

Goldwash, Nevada
December 24th

> *O holy night!*
> *The stars are brightly shining...*

W ould you turn off that Christmas crap and help me clean up all this ..." A déjà vu gave me pause in the midst of throwing a wet rag at my cousin Buffalo, who nursed a mug of beer at the end of the bar.

Buffalo frowned at me over his glass. "Jeez, Montana, can't you let a man enjoy a nostalgic moment? Where's your—"

"Holiday spirit?" I finished for him, feeling like I was rehearsing for a play I knew from memory. Something was supposed to come next about Brunhilda, Buffalo's fat bulldog, who lay splayed on her belly next to his bar stool snoring, but I changed it up. "I lost it when Joel left town."

The bastard broke my heart and months later it still sat like a cold, cracked piece of granite in my chest.

I dragged a bucket of sudsy, ammonia-smelling water around to the front of the bar, pulling the stools out on each side of Buffalo, only to realize there wasn't anything to mop up, except peanut shells. Hadn't something been spilled here? Weird.

"I'm closing the bar early tonight," I told Buffalo. "You

want to come back to my place and hang out for a while? Watch a movie? I think the Western channel is having a Clint Eastwood marathon."

Buffalo wiped the beer foam moustache from his upper lip. "Sure, if you don't mind me bringing Brunhilda. I hate to leave her alone on Christmas Eve."

"Are you afraid she'll actually wake up this year for Christmas?" His dog stirred only long enough to snarfle down food, I swore.

He grinned and reached down to scratch Brunhilda's head between her fake reindeer antlers. "She'll perk up. Santa brought her a special bone."

Brunhilda's ears twitched at the word *bone*, but that was the only sign of life.

"I'm not interfering with any plans with your girlfriend, am I?" I asked.

"Didn't you hear? We split up. She's knocking boots with my neighbor now."

"Oh." How had I missed that in this one-horse town? I really needed to get my head out of the sand and get back to living. "Sorry."

"Don't be." He waved me off. "He has pigs. Her constant squealing doesn't faze him."

That made me smile. "Do you think you'll ever find a nice woman, settle down, raise a couple of baby buffalos? You're not getting any younger, you know." Buffalo had two years on my thirty-six.

"Nope. I've told you my thoughts about monogamy and matrimony too many times to count."

"What happened with your parents isn't genetic, you know. Marriages don't have to involve flying cast iron skillets and burning pickups. Look at my parents. They were married for almost forty years." And then Momma got sick and all of our lives went to hell in a handcart.

Buffalo slurped his beer. "Yeah, well you're not setting

the best example for happily ever after. First, you shacked up with a three-timin' rodeo clown, then you married a killer, and *then* you hooked up with Joel Andersen, of all guys. You're like the pin-up girl for *Fucked-Up Life* magazine."

He had a point, but I didn't need him needling me with it. "Kiss my pin-up ass." I picked up the wet rag and whipped it at him.

He dodged it, chuckling.

"So marriage isn't for me," I said. "But that doesn't mean you can't make a go of it."

"Monty, dear, you may not know a thing about picking the right guy, but you sure throw one hell of a Christmas party."

He was changing the subject, as he so often did when I tried to bring up his future love life for anything other than his damned dog.

"I think this party was our best since Momma ran the bar," I said, going along with him. Tonight's drunken merriment replayed in my head as I kicked the mop bucket to the corner, including slurred caroling, random sloppy kisses, and a marriage proposal from a lonely widowed rancher who had a huge spread east of town. Too bad he was a leftover from the Paleozoic era.

I reached up to remove some tinsel hanging from the ceiling fan and the telephone hanging on the wall behind the bar rang. I jogged over to grab it then hesitated with my hand on the receiver. I'd gotten a rash of creepy calls lately, filled with heavy breathing and this skin-crawling, undecipherable whispering.

When I'd told Buffalo about the calls, he'd pushed me to tell the sheriff, but I'd resisted because the local law dog also happened to be Joel's brother. While I liked to think my hesitation had more to do with not letting some heavy breather bully me into running with my tail between my legs, I had no doubt that my pride figured into the mix.

"I'm not sure if you know this," Buffalo said, "but you need to actually pick up the receiver to make the phone stop ringing."

I flipped him off and lifted the handset. "The Ugly Rooster," I said, using my usual greeting.

A thick silence came through the line, sounding as if I'd tuned into some empty airspace out over one of the government's testing ranges. I'd almost rather have the breathing. After the count of three, I hung up.

"Dead," I answered Buffalo's wrinkled brow. I double-checked to make sure the 12-gauge shotgun I'd brought from home earlier this week was still under the counter.

The bell over the front door jingled, making me jerk in surprise, raising the shotgun in reaction.

Buffalo hollered over his shoulder, "Bar's closed."

"I disagree." The deep voice nearly made me choke on my tongue.

I gripped the shotgun, wishing I'd loaded it with rock salt instead of slugs.

"You brought out your big gun to welcome me home?" Joel Andersen asked, closing the door on the wailing groan of the Nevada winter wind. "I'm flattered."

I put the shotgun down on the bar before I did something stupid like shoot Joel in the toe.

"Well, well, well," Buffalo said, his tone low. "Would ya look at that—the old man's back in town." He cocked an eyebrow at me. "Am I leavin'?"

"Stay," I said, my gaze focused on Joel as he crossed the bar floor, shucking his thick coat along the way. He must have thought he was staying, too. He was mistaken.

Joel was carrying, as usual, his Colt .45 riding in his shoulder holster.

Before I sent him back out into the cold winter night, I took a moment to drink in the sight of his wind-ruffled black hair, stubble-covered square jaw, and bright green eyes. My heartbeat ratcheted, my core cranked up the heat, and my mouth went dry.

Ah, damn. Hell was coming to Christmas.

Joel cozied up to the bar.

I crossed my arms over my chest. "Like Buffalo said, the bar's closed."

"I heard him, Shooter." My childhood nickname rolled off his tongue like he'd never deserted town and left me face down in a mud puddle.

He patted Buffalo on the back. "Hey Buff, I'm hanging around for a bit. Want some help with fixing up the ol' Goldwash Grand?"

Hanging around for a bit? How long was a bit? More importantly, why was Joel here? No, even more worrisome, how was I going to keep from ending up in his bed when just the sight of him had me wanting to vault the bar, lay him out with my fists, and then have my merry naked way with him?

Criminy, I'd seen centipedes with more backbone than I had when it came to the green-eyed devil in front of me.

"Free labor? You're hired." Buffalo snuck a glance my way. "But aren't you gonna miss the wild Vegas nightlife?"

"No," Joel answered Buffalo, but his green eyes held mine captive, a fire burning in their depths that practically made my skin crackle from the heat. "The nightlife here is much wilder."

I took a step back before I got seared. "What do you want, Joel?" I asked, not mincing words.

His gaze dropped to the front of my shirt. "I need to talk to you, Montana."

My body felt the invisible pull that was always there between us, lassoing me, tugging me in.

I grabbed a bottle of whiskey from the shelf, needing something to scrub the taste of Joel off my mind. "Here's the deal," I said, pouring myself a shot. "I spent the last few months trying to work you out of my system." I tossed back the amber liquid, which burned all of the way down, firing me up. "I'll be damned if you get to just walk back into my life and fuck me over again."

The phone rang. I yanked the receiver off the wall. "What?"

I heard heavy breathing.

"What the hell do you want, damn it?"

"Mon-taaan-na," a voice whispered.

I felt my eyes widen in surprise. I looked at Buffalo, who watched me, his focus unwavering.

"What?" I whispered back, my voice hiding down in my throat.

"I see you when you're sleeping."

I opened my mouth, but nothing came out. There was something about the voice I recognized, something in the way he'd said my name, all sing-songy like.

"I know when you're awake," he paused between each line, letting them sink in.

My hand started to tremble.

"Who is it?" Joel asked.

"I know when you've been bad, Mon-taaan-na." There it was again. "And you've been a very bad girl."

"Who is this?" I voiced, my words sounding far away.

"Give me the phone," Joel said, coming around the bar.

"It's time for you to be punished," the creep whispered. "And when I'm done, you'll wish you were—"

Joel ripped the receiver from my hand. "Who is this?" he spoke into the phone.

I took several steps back, the creep's words replaying in my head, sparking that déjà vu again.

Joel hung up the phone and turned to me. "What did he say?"

Then it hit me, an echo from the past. I knew that

voice!

The fear gripping my lungs tightened in rage. "No!" I shoved past Joel, yanking the phone off the wall and throwing it on the floor where I stomped on it with my boot heel.

"Montana!" Joel grabbed me by the shoulders. "Stop it."

I broke his hold, snatching up my 12-gauge. "Damn you, Joel."

"What did I do?"

I back-stepped toward the swinging doors, glaring at him. "You came here to stop me."

"From what?" Buffalo asked, half off his bar stool.

"Montana, give me the shotgun," Joel took a step toward me, holding out his hand palm up.

"From what?" Buffalo asked again.

I spared him a frown. "From killing that son of a bitch I married."

Joel took another step toward me. "Hand over your weapon before you hurt someone."

"Negative, *Detective* Andersen," I said in his cop lingo. "You need to get out of my bar before I fill you full of holes, too." I glanced at Buffalo. "Lock the door on your way out, would ya?"

Without another word, I grabbed the bottle of whiskey, leaned my shotgun over my shoulder, and shoved through the swinging half-doors that led back to my office.

New Christmas Eve plan—prepare for a showdown with that rotten bastard I'd divorced and put behind bars for killing his business partner. I was done cowering at his threats.

"Montana," Joel called from behind me. "Come back to me."

"Go to hell!" I stepped through my office doorway.

He didn't listen, following on my boot heels, shutting

the door behind him and locking it.

I slammed the bottle of whiskey down on my desk, spilling some on the get-well cards stacked on it. "Andersen, your inability to follow my directions has always pissed me off."

"Put the shotgun down." He grabbed the 12-gauge from me, using it to tug me toward him.

"I'm done running scared."

"Good. Give me your gun."

"You have your own. Why do you need mine?"

"Two reasons—first, because you make me sweaty when you are swinging this thing around." I let him take it from me. He placed it gently on the desk, the muzzle facing away from us, and then laid his Colt .45 next to it. "Second, because I can't concentrate on talking to you when you have that in your hands."

"We said all there was to say months ago."

"You're right." He grabbed me by the front of my T-shirt, yanked me into him, and planted a hard kiss on my mouth. "Take off your pants."

I glared up at him. "You think you can come slamming into town and land right back between my legs?"

"A man can hope."

"You have a big set of balls, Joel Andersen."

He grinned and buried his fingers in my hair, backing me into the desk. "You can admire those later."

I met his lips mid-way this time, thirsty for a drink of him, tearing his shirt out of his jeans to touch the flesh I'd only been able to think about for way too long. He groaned when I raked my nails over his stomach, his mouth savoring mine, exploring then ravaging again. I clutched his back and plastered myself against him, soaking him up like a dry lakebed.

He stepped back long enough to peel my T-shirt off and toss it on the floor. In between kisses, his flannel shirt followed, then his thermal undershirt.

"Joel," I said when he fell back onto my silver couch and pulled me down so I straddled him. "You have to stop."

"Why?" he asked, his hands spanning my hips.

His lips trailed down between my breasts, his touch electrifying, lighting chills along the way.

"Because ..." I started, and then moaned when his teeth nipped me through my bra cup.

My hands held him against me, as my body arched toward him and his tongue teased me through the cotton.

I closed my eyes, trying to focus on what I was trying to spit out. "Because ..."

He shifted me on his lap, adjusting so that his rough edges dug into my soft spots. "Damn, I missed you, Shooter."

I moaned under the gully wash of sensations I'd only dreamed about for months, my body coming to life like the desert after a spring gusher. The heat of his mouth left my breast then coolness followed when he blew on the damp cotton.

I shivered, closing my eyes, and finally found the end of my sentence. "Because you left me."

He stilled under my body. "Montana, open those big blue eyes for a moment."

I did, frowning down at him. His chest rose and fell rapidly, his face taut, his need shining bright in his green gaze.

"I came back here tonight to tell you that your ex-husband escaped from prison a week ago."

I blinked. "That explains the strange calls I've been getting all week."

"We've had an APB out for him since he disappeared." He popped open the button of my jeans. "Yesterday, a convenience store owner down in Beatty recognized him and called the cops, but he slipped by them."

"You sure it was him?"

"He bought unfiltered cigarettes, black licorice, and orange soda pop."

That was him all right. "So you're here on my couch on official police business?"

"Yes," he said. His hand slipped inside of my jeans, his fingers dipping below the elastic waist of my panties.

"Well, I hope you have a warrant to get into my underwear."

His grin lit his face with a wicked glow. "I sure do. It's in my pants. Why don't you reach down in my front left pocket and grab it."

"Oh, no, Mr. Lawman. I've fallen for that trick with you before. It ended with me up against the side of your car with my bare ass to the wind."

"What can I say? It's my job to search for hidden weapons. On a night as dark as that one, I had to check out every single one of your nooks and crannies."

I rocked my hips, rubbing against him. "You should be careful what you search for. If I remember correctly, you're the one who ended up cuffed to your door handle that night with your pants around your ankles."

He chuckled. "Good thing Rick was on duty. He still cries like a girl when he laughs his way through that story."

I leaned down and ravished his mouth, slow and sultry, basking in the pre-glow of what his hips were promising to deliver.

He unhooked my bra single-handedly while I was distracted, his other palm still gripping my hips, keeping me tight against him. "Montana, sweetheart?"

"Mmmm?" I managed to get out while his hand got reacquainted with my bared breast.

"When I walked in that door tonight and saw you behind the bar all full of spitfire and sparks, I changed my mind about something."

"About what?"

He pressed harder against me, the friction seeming to light his firecracker as much as it did mine. "Walking away."

"From Goldwash?"

"From you." His mouth took the place of his hand on my breast, his tongue flicking, while both hands lifted me enough to wrestle my jeans and underwear down over my hips. His pants hit the floor next.

"Just like that?" I halted the show, glaring down at him as he shifted free of his briefs. "You come back here and tell me you've changed your mind and I'm supposed to drop everything and let you back into my heart."

"No. Just like this." He pulled me down onto him, watching my face as he slid all of the way in, then out and in again ever so slowly, this time staying put and drawing my hips toward him.

"Oh," I whispered, grasping his shoulders, arching my back to help him hit the spot, all of the spots. "Just like that."

He let his head lean back against the couch cushion, watching me from beneath lowered lashes. "You have no idea how damned sexy you look right now riding me with your hair tangled and your skin glowing."

"We always were good at sex," I said between heavy breaths. "It's the talking where we get stuck in the mud."

"We're doing fine right now."

"That's because you get all chatty when you're inside of me. You're the only guy I've ever been with who has conversations during sex."

"How many guys are we talking about again?"

"Barely enough to shake a stick at."

"Good." He groaned and sat forward, closing the gap between us. "Damn, you're always so wet." He shifted me so that we fit even closer, helping me move faster. "Walking out on you was the hardest thing I ever did."

The dust devil of need inside of me swirled faster, higher. "Then why did you?"

Joel picked up the momentum, seeming to sense that I wasn't going to last much longer. "Because you wouldn't marry me."

I growled at the ceiling. "It's just a piece of paper. We didn't need it to tell us what we already knew."

"You're right. We didn't need it, but I wanted it. I wanted you."

"You had me, Joel." I reached down behind me and scraped my fingernails up his thighs. "Like you do right now."

He let go of my hips, his fingers occupied themselves in other creative ways.

"Tell me what you need." His thumbs circled and rubbed, making me writhe with want.

"I need you to shut up and take me the rest of the way."

"I love it when you boss me around, Shooter," he said in a gravelly voice.

Without another word, he massaged and strummed all of the right buttons and knobs until I pulsed around him, squeezing him tight, making him cuss and shudder shortly after me.

I let my forehead rest on his shoulder, catching my breath, peeking at him out of the corner of my eye.

Joel stared at the ceiling, his Adam's apple bobbing every few seconds as he caught his breath. "Call me old fashioned, sweetheart," he said without looking at me, "but I wanted the vows. The cake, the rings, a 'wife' to sleep next to every night."

Damn it, why did he have to ruin my afterglow with more talk of marriage. I rolled off him, grabbing my underwear off the floor. "You know I have a bad track record, Joel."

"Stop living in the past. Look at what you have right here in front of you."

I did. Warmth bubbled in my chest. Damn he was one big gorgeous chunk of flesh and bones. "I left a bite mark on your shoulder again."

He touched the red spot, staring up at me. "I don't want to live without you anymore. Come back to me, Montana."

I pulled up my jeans and buttoned them, considering his words.

Let's see, I could spend the rest of my life lonely and miserable and pining for the sexy stud sprawled on my couch, or I could have him in my bed every night, talking about how much he adores me while loving me up and down and all around.

There was no way in hell I was going to stumble back into the wasteland I'd lived in the last few months.

I grabbed my shirt from the floor, skipping the bra. "Okay," I told him and unlocked the door, hauling it open. "Stay here while I make sure I'm all shut up for the night."

"*Okay?*" he asked, adjusting himself and reaching for his jeans. "What do you mean *okay*? Okay you'll come back or okay you'll marry me this time?"

Something thudded out front.

I froze, straining to catch more. "Did you hear that?"

"Hear what?" Joel said, buttoning his fly.

Another thud resounded, followed by a grunt and a crash. *Buffalo!*

"That." I grabbed my shotgun, running out the door and cocking my gun on the race down the hall.

"Montana," Joel hollered still inside my office. "Come back to me."

Why did he keep saying that?

I hesitated outside the swinging doors, then leaned down and scrambled over behind the bar.

The room was dark, all lights off, even the beer lights I

usually left on in the windows. The dim hall light seeped through the swinging doors, offering a feeble glow. I pressed my back against the bar, waiting for my eyes to adjust, listening for any sounds that would clue me into the situation.

Then I heard it, the labored breathing in the darkness.

I needed to know if Buff was okay, but didn't want to give my position away. I heard a scuff, then a low groan.

"Buffalo?" I whispered. "Are you okay?"

Nobody answered. *Shit!*

Where in the hell was Joel? I could use a cop right about now.

Then again, maybe I was all hopped up on adrenaline and making more out of this than it was. Maybe Buffalo was just closing up shop and tripped over that damned dog of his, making the thud and crash sounds I'd heard, knocking himself out on the way down.

But why were my beer lights off? Buffalo knew I liked to leave them on all night.

A shout came from the other side of the swinging doors—Joel's voice, sounding like he'd told someone to freeze.

A gunshot echoed down the hallway.

I gasped in surprise then covered my mouth. *Joel?*

My heart pounded. I wanted to go back there, make sure he was okay, but I couldn't just go swinging in like Rooster Cogburn.

Another groan came from somewhere in the darkness.

Damn it, I wasn't going to sit here forever and wait for the sun to come up.

Clutching the shotgun in one hand, I inched across the floor on my butt toward the stool where I'd last seen Buffalo, keeping my boots from thudding on the wood and giving away my location.

The dim light trickling in from the hall went dark,

pitching me into complete blackness.

My breath came fast. I gasped for oxygen as panic hogtied my lungs. I scooted under the bar, my palms covered with dirt and pieces of peanut shells. The smells of old varnish and dust offered no comfort in the darkness.

I heard a scuff of a boot come from the side of the room I'd just left, the creak of a floorboard followed.

Someone else had joined the party. Was it Joel, or whoever he'd faced off with down the hall?

A snore rattled out right next to me and I almost peed my pants. A snuffle followed, then a grunt as Brunhilda made herself comfortable in the darkness. I reached out and felt for her, my fingers connecting with her soft, pudgy tummy. She let out what sounded like a squeaking yawn and wiggled closer to my hand.

The relief of knowing she was in here with me was pushed aside by the knowledge that it meant Buffalo was here, too. Somewhere in the darkness. Probably hurt.

I counted to ten, then twenty, listening to the creaking of the roof overhead, the muffled wail of the wind howling outside. Someone was going to have to get things rolling or we could be stuck in a Mexican standoff all night.

I got into a squatting position so I could make a dash, if needed, and then called out loud and clear, "Buffalo? Are you in here?"

"Hey, baby," a scratchy voice from my checkered past said in the darkness. "I've been waiting in here for you to welcome me home with open arms."

Shit! My ex was here, and I doubted he'd brought presents or fruitcake.

"What did you do to Buffalo?" I asked.

"Let's just say that good ol' Buff had a little accident."

It sounded like he was in the back east corner of the room, near the pool table and old juke box. "If you hurt Buffalo, I'm going to rip off your balls and stuff them down your throat right after I fill you full of hot lead."

"I always loved it when you talked dirty to me, baby."

I crawled over Brunhilda, slinking toward the other end of the bar, and ran my hand up the wall to where one of the two lights switches was located for my over-the-bar lights. If I were going to shoot, I needed to see where so I didn't hit Buffalo by accident. Again.

One of my knees popped as I stood up. *Damn it!*

"I can hear you moving, baby, and I saw that shotgun when you snuck in here. Why don't you just put the gun down and you and I can have us a nice little walk down memory lane."

I took a deep breath, aimed the barrel in his direction, and flicked the light switch on.

There he was behind the pool table, next to the juke box, right where I'd pictured the rotten bastard. I pulled the trigger.

A boom echoed through the room. Followed by a volley of shots as he ducked behind the pool table, popping up to fire back with what looked like a Glock.

I squatted on the floor, covering my head when the huge mirror behind me exploded, coating me with glass shards.

I had to get back behind the bar, take cover. Flicking off the lights again, I scrambled blindly through the darkness in a squat run toward the swinging doors.

Shots rang out so loud that I couldn't tell from where they'd come. I heard something whiz by my ear and winced. Wood splintered close by.

My boot connected with something that felt like a rolled up carpet.

Brunhilda yipped and barked when I tripped over her.

Another shot fired, and pain flared through my head just above my ear as I stumbled. My shotgun went off as I fell flat on my back onto the floor, jerking free of my hands in recoil.

I lay there, staring into the darkness, my ears ringing as I struggled to hear. My head throbbed on the left side like a son of a bitch.

Something warm pooled in my ear, trickling down my neck. I touched it—too thick and slippery to be alcohol. Blood. It was blood. My blood? That would explain the burning pain on the side of my head. Was I shot?

I coughed on the gunpowder burning the back of my throat.

"Montana," Joel called. His voice sounded miles away, like we stood on opposite ridges. "Montana!"

Relief made my limbs feel like Jell-O. Thank the heavens, he was still alive.

"Montana, where are you?"

I heard footfalls on the wood floor.

Several more shots were fired.

"No, Joel!" I screamed. He was going to get himself killed trying to get to me.

I struggled to my feet, but my head felt like a helium balloon, floating away. I swayed to the left.

A shot rang out, winging my shoulder, stinging like hell.

My boots slipped on the blood or peanut shells or both. I teetered to the right, the blackness swirling around me, and fell, that throbbing left side of my skull connecting with something hard on the way down.

I lay there for several heartbeats, my cheek on the gritty wood floor, pain making me nauseated.

The front door crashed open.

Lights flickered on overhead.

There were several shouts and then the sound of scuffling, wood breaking, grunts and groans.

A pair of scuffed up cowboy boots filled my vision.

Then I closed my eyes and let the black Nevada night blow me away.

Cottontop Flats, Nevada
December 26th

Should auld acquaintance be forgot
And never brought to mind...

I opened my eyes, blinking in the flickering glow of the light from the television secured to the wall at the end of my hospital bed. Someone needed to change the channel and get that damned depressing song off the boob-tube. It was making the side of my head throb. I tried to swallow. Criminy, my mouth was dry. My throat felt like it'd been bored out with a diamond-studded ...

Wait a second! Hospital bed? My gaze darted around the shadow-filled room, taking in the half-eaten Jell-O on the tray next to me, the needle jammed into my arm, the little winged pigs covering my cotton gown, the bandage on my left shoulder, and the toilet with handles through the half-open bathroom door.

The sound of a half-snore followed by a grunt brought my focus back to the dark-haired man who slept leaning partway across the right side of my bed, using my hip as a makeshift cushion. Joel's wavy black hair shielded one of his eyes, his jaw was covered with at least two days' worth of stubble.

I reached down with my right arm and sank my fingers into his hair, lifting his head up a couple of inches.

One emerald green eye opened, then the other.

I let go of his hair. "Wake up and tell me I killed the

bastard," I said, my voice hoarse from lack of use.

"Sorry, Shooter. You missed." He stood and stretched. His gaze traveled over my face, assessing.

"Water?" I asked. He grabbed a pitcher from the tray and poured some in a cup, holding me up while I drank.

With his help, I sank back into the pillow, wincing from a bolt of pain in my shoulder. "Did I even come close?"

"No. I did, though." He sat on the bed, leaning over me. His fingers traced my face, like he was memorizing every bump and hollow. "He won't be bothering you ever again."

"Damn it, Joel. That was supposed to give me closure after the years of hell he put me through."

"Well, if it makes you feel any better, you did blow a hole in the jukebox."

"What about Buffalo?"

He scooted closer. "He has a broken arm from tackling your ex."

"Before you shot him?"

"After."

"Brunhilda?"

"Fat and happy, as usual."

"You?"

"Fit as a fiddle." He squeezed my hand. "You, on the other hand, had a bullet leave a groove in the left side of your skull and another rip a hole through the meat on the outside of your left shoulder. Do you remember anything from that night?"

I thought about the dream that had kept replaying in my head, the details all blurred together. "I remember blood. A lot of blood."

"Head wounds are like that. You had to get staples."

That explained the throbbing on that side of my head. "I remember sex in my office."

He grinned wide. "You rode me like a rodeo queen. I'm

going to need a repeat of that. I'm thinking chaps and a thong, maybe some tassels and spurs."

I licked my dry lips. "But what am *I* gonna wear?"

He laughed, leaning down to kiss my nose. "What else do you remember, sweetheart?"

"Hitting my head."

"You nearly cracked the bar with your thick skull when you fell. The lump blossomed into a pretty purple bruise."

"How long have I been out?"

"Two days after the ambulance ride here. At first they kept you out in order to get you all patched up. Then you went in and out of consciousness thanks to the pain meds, but mostly out."

"Where's here?"

"The regional hospital in Cottontop Flats."

"My dad?"

"He's resting at a hotel nearby."

I closed my eyes for a moment, something niggling at my memory of it all. "I remember you telling someone to freeze."

"Your ex wasn't alone. His girlfriend snuck in the back door. She took off when I drew on her. Rick tracked her down, found her hiding in the boarded up old high school, and locked her up. She's going to go away for a long time."

I reached up and touched the left side of my head, grimacing as I brushed over the staples and shaved hair. "I tripped over that damned dog."

"That 'damned dog' probably saved your life. You should have seen all of the bullet holes in the bar."

"Buffalo will probably want to have a parade for his heroic mutt."

Joel's smile flat-lined. "You scared me on the ride here, Shooter. With all of that blood you lost, I was afraid you wouldn't come back to me."

Come back to me, Montana.

That explained why he kept saying that in my dreams. My throat tightened. Careful not to jar my shoulder, I scooted over, patting the bed next to me.

He glanced at the door then climbed in next to me, mindful of the needle in my arm. He brushed his beard stubble over my forehead as he held me close. "You missed Christmas."

"You'll have to make it up to me at New Year's."

"It's a deal. Do you remember saying you'd marry me?"

It was my turn to laugh. "Good try, Andersen."

"Laugh it up, Montana, but Santa left you a little package under the tree."

"Isn't that sweet," I said, still smiling. "But Santa knows I like my packages big." I reached down and squeezed him through his fly. "This will do me just fine."

His surprised cough morphed into a raspy chuckle. "I can't believe I'm in love with such a salty wench." The tender brush of his lips over my temple smoothed away the last burrs of my resistance.

"Okay," I said, staring up at the television as Clint Eastwood rode off into the horizon.

"Okay what?"

"I'll wear your ring."

He sat up, gaping down at me. "No shit?"

"No shit." I reached up and ran my knuckles over his scruff. "But I'm keeping The Ugly Rooster."

He grinned. "You'll have to make moving back worth my while." He bent down, his lips feathering over my face. His hand traced my contours through the cotton pig-covered gown. "Let's start with those tassels and spurs."

I caught his roving hand and held it over my heart. "Don't forget the chaps and thong."

"Trust me, Shooter, I won't. I think I'll include them in my wedding vow."

The End ...for now.

More Books by Ann

Books in the Deadwood Mystery Series

WINNER of the 2010 Daphne du Maurier Award for Excellence in Mystery/Suspense

WINNER of the 2011 Romance Writers of America® Golden Heart Award for Best Novel with Strong Romantic Elements

Welcome to Deadwood—the Ann Charles version. The world I have created is a blend of present day and past, of fiction and non-fiction. What's real and what isn't is for you to determine as the series develops, the characters evolve, and I write the stories line by line. I will tell you one thing about the series—it's going to run on for quite a while, and Violet Parker will have to hang on and persevere through the crazy adventures I have planned for her. Poor, poor Violet. It's a good thing she has a lot of gumption to keep her going!

Short Stories from Ann's
Deadwood Mystery Series

The Deadwood Shorts collection includes short stories featuring the characters of the Deadwood Mystery series.

Each tale not only explains more of Violet's history, but also gives a little history of the other characters you know and love from the series. Rather than filling the main novels in the series with these short side stories, I've put them into a growing Deadwood Shorts collection for more reading fun.

The Dig Site Mystery Series

From the award-winning author of the Deadwood Mystery Series comes the adventurous and suspense-filled Dig Site Mystery series starring Violet Parker's brother, Quint.

"Intelligent and witty characters and an exotic mystery set in an archeology dig among Maya ruins—don't miss this entertaining adventure!"

~Pamela Beason, Author of the
Summer Westin Mysteries & the Neema Mysteries

Welcome to the jungle—the steamy Maya jungle that is, filled with ancient ruins, deadly secrets, and quirky characters. Quint Parker, renowned photojournalist (and lousy amateur detective), is in for a whirlwind of adventure and suspense as he and archaeologist Dr. Angelica Garcia get tangled up in mysteries from the past and present in exotic dig sites. Loaded with action and laughs, along with all sorts of steamy heat, these two will keep you sweating along with them as they do their best to make it out of the jungle alive in every book.

The Jackrabbit Junction Mystery Series

Bestseller in Women Sleuth Mystery and Romantic Suspense

Welcome to the Dancing Winnebagos RV Park. Down here in Jackrabbit Junction, Arizona, Claire Morgan and her rabble-rousing sisters are really good at getting into trouble—BIG trouble (the land your butt in jail kind of trouble). This rowdy, laugh-aloud mystery series is packed with action, suspense, adventure, and relationship snafus. Full of colorful characters and twisted up plots, the stories of the Morgan sisters will keep you wondering what kind of a screwball mess they are going to land in next.

Ann Charles is a USA Today Bestselling author who writes award-winning mysteries that are splashed with humor, romance, and whatever else she feels like throwing into the mix. When she is not dabbling in fiction, arm-wrestling with her children, attempting to seduce her husband, or arguing with her sassy cat, she is daydreaming of lounging poolside at a fancy resort with a blended margarita in one hand and a great book in the other.

Facebook (Personal Page):
http://www.facebook.com/ann.charles.author

Facebook (Author Page):
http://www.facebook.com/pages/Ann-Charles/37302789804?ref=share

Twitter (as Ann W. Charles):
http://twitter.com/AnnWCharles

Ann Charles Website:
http://www.anncharles.com